WHILE THE JURY WAITS

Dr. Tony Vercillo

Copyright © 2025

All Rights Reserved

Also by Dr. Tony Vercillo

Launch It: From Idea to the Store Shelf

Using your Supply Chain as a Competitive Weapon

Death by Media

Dedication

This novel is dedicated to my amazing children and our extended family. For Anthony, Darien, and Nicolas…you are my life and my purpose for living!

Acknowledgements

There are many people I want to acknowledge for their help or inspiration. I want to thank my editors and their support team.

Special thanks to John Thyne, my mentor and dear friend, for shaping me into the man I am today. If it were not for John, I'd still be doing manual labor in Brooklyn.

I want to acknowledge my children for their never-ending support and love.

And finally, I want to thank all my students who kept me on my toes and provided years of enjoyment.

About the Author

Dr. Tony Vercillo is a 30-year veteran in the Product Marketing and Distribution industry. He has a Doctorate in Marketing Management, with special emphasis on Global Marketing Strategies (Summa Cum Laude). He also received his MBA in Leadership and Human Behavior. He is a highly sought-after public speaker known for his *"infectious enthusiasm."*

Dr. Vercillo has been an Author for more than 30 years in the non-fiction arena. He always dreamt of dabbling in the fiction world, and this work is his first foray into the exciting world of novels.

Dr. Vercillo has served as a Senior-Level Manager and Vice President for PepsiCo and a third-party supply-chain firm. He is currently the CEO of a major kosher food service company in New Jersey. He also recently retired from teaching Global Marketing Strategy and Supply Chain Theory at California State University. His passion in life is teaching and coaching, and he has spent the last 20 years fulfilling that dream.

You can contact Dr. Vercillo on YouTube (Ask the Doc: Life Lessons Podcast) or at www.doclifelessons.com

Preface

Prior to writing this book, I dabbled in the world of non-fiction. This is my first attempt at writing a work of fiction. The inspiration for this work was driven by an intense desire to prove I could do it, that is, write a fiction novel. My students, family, and friends all encouraged me to take a shot at writing something outside my comfort zone.

Although I probably have delusions of grandeur, I also wanted to write a tome that was made for TV and the Big Screen. We shall see if I am overreaching.

Another reason for writing this novel is my obsession with TV courtroom drama. I have always said that, given another life, I would strive to become a defense attorney.

It is my sincere hope that you share my enthusiasm for this work. And remember, at the core of this work is the presumption that people are innocent until proven guilty.

Contents

Part 1: The Charmer's Conundrum 1
Chapter 1: Courtroom Charisma 2
Chapter 2: An Unexpected Turn 14
Chapter 3: Shadows of Doubt 20
Chapter 4: Unveiling Shadows 38
Chapter 5: The Whispers in Twilight...59
Chapter 6: The Eclipse of Revelations..71
Chapter 7: The Shadows of Ravenbrook 85
Chapter 8: Threads of Deception 94
Chapter 9: The Rusted Clue 105
Chapter 10: The Masked Agenda..114
Chapter 11: Web of Lies 124
Chapter 12: Truth or Consequences..134
Chapter 13: Echoes of Rain and Justice..................................145
Chapter 14: Blood Stains and Broken Codes..........................156
Chapter 15: Tipping the Scales 168
Chapter 16: The Crossroads 177
Chapter 17: Pieces of the Puzzle..191
Chapter 18: A Trial of Nerves..202
Chapter 19: The Veiled Truth 217
Chapter 20: The Final Judgment 228

Part 1: The Charmer's Conundrum

Sometimes, it's not the person who changes; it's the mask that falls off.

—Mhaj Porras

Chapter 1: Courtroom Charisma

In the bustling heart of the city, Giuseppe "Gio" Rossi sauntered down the crowded streets with an air of unapologetic confidence. He reveled in the rhythm of the city that mirrored the beat of his own pulsating ego. This was his stage, and he was the lead performer in the grand theatrical production of his life.

Gio's perfectly styled hair caught the sunlight as he strolled, his dapper suit attracting admiring glances from passersby. He could feel eyes following him, and he relished in the silent acknowledgment of his magnetic charm. The world was his audience, and he played to it with every calculated step.

Approaching the entrance of his office building, Gio smirked at the thought of the day's conquests awaiting him. He made his way to his own office and stopped before the door.

The small, unassuming sign on the door read *"G. Rossi, Attorney at Law,"* a modest title for a man of his stature. With a flick of his wrist, he pushed the door open, entering the realm of his legal kingdom.

The air inside was laced with the faint scent of expensive cologne, a signature fragrance that lingered long after he had passed through. The office was compact, but Gio had transformed it into a lavish sanctuary that reflected his taste for the finer things in life. Deep mahogany furniture exuded an aura of sophistication, and the walls were adorned with framed accolades and photographs capturing moments of triumph in the courtroom.

As he traversed the space, his fingers brushed against the spines of leather-bound law books that stood proudly on the shelves. They were relics of a time when he believed legal knowledge was a necessity, but now they served as mere decorations. His journey from earnest student to charismatic showman was a quick one since he never really believed he needed to put in work to win people over. That was all that law was—winning people over. These books had not been opened since his law school days, but he kept them lined up on the shelf in order of height and color because it made his clients trust him more. He was sure that none of them could even understand the titles of the books, let alone the content, but they looked fancy and serious.

His desk, an expansive slab of polished wood, bore the weight of a few strategically placed trinkets—a gold-plated pen, a photograph of Gio with a renowned judge, and a crystal paperweight that caught the light in a dazzling dance. The windows offered a glimpse of the city below, a constant reminder of the chaos he navigated with finesse.

Seating himself behind the desk, Gio flipped on the desk lamp, casting a warm glow over the disorganized chaos of paperwork. He ran a hand through his impeccably groomed hair, gazing at his reflection in a sleek mirror on the wall. His self-assured smile lingered as he surveyed the domain he had crafted.

An armed robbery case loomed on the periphery of his thoughts, a mere blip on his radar of legal conquests. With an audacious flick of his wrist, he opened the drawer and retrieved a set of notes, scrawled with swift strokes of his pen. Five minutes had been all it took to craft a narrative that would sway the court in his favor.

A sly grin played on his lips as he reveled in the simplicity of the task at hand. Armed robbery, a petty crime, was a puzzle waiting to be solved by his cunning mind.

As he gathered the notes, the door to his office swung open, revealing his elegantly dressed secretary. Her eyes met his as she gestured for him to meet his client. Other lawyers would typically come hours before their case was to be presented so as to prepare for the task ahead. But, for Gio, this was no task at all. He was sure he would be in and out of that courtroom in minutes, shaking his client's hand and being paid. Gio Rossi was not just an attorney; he was a force of nature.

The attractive secretary exited, leaving the door open. Gio watched as she walked away and took a seat at her own desk. With a final glance around the room, he rose from his seat, leaving the office to embrace the chaos of the legal battlefield. The city awaited his presence and armed with his charisma and a few carefully chosen words, he was ready to conquer yet another courtroom.

Under the midday sun, Giuseppe "Gio" Rossi stepped out of his office, the polished marble floors echoing the confident click of his Italian leather shoes. He sauntered toward the parking lot with the self-assured swagger that defined him. The city's rhythm seemed to sync with his every step, evidence of the undeniable charisma that trailed in his wake.

Approaching his pride and joy, a sleek charcoal-gray luxury car, Gio couldn't help but admire the reflection of his meticulously dressed self in the tinted windows. The vehicle, a symbol of his success, glistened in the sun. A ton of people stopped and asked about it, and he caught multiple people taking pictures with it, too; beautiful girls sat on the hood posing and taking pictures. He was still paying off the car and would be for the next few years, but for a man of his importance, such financial details were inconsequential compared to the image he projected.

The car, a high-end model that turned heads as it glided down the streets, showed Gio's taste for the finer things in life. Its polished exterior gleamed under the sunlight, and the leather interior exuded a scent of opulence that matched his own. He knew the importance of making an entrance, and the car served as an extension of his persona.

Sliding into the driver's seat with practiced ease, Gio adjusted the leather-clad steering wheel to his liking. His fingers traced the smooth surface, a tactile reminder of the luxury he had earned. He turned his key, and the engine roared to life.

The dapper lawyer meticulously adjusted his tailored suit, ensuring every crease fell just right. His crisp white shirt accentuated the tan of his Italian skin, and the silk tie, carefully chosen to exude both power and elegance, hung with deliberate nonchalance. The suit itself, a charcoal-gray masterpiece, clung to his frame in a way that showcased his muscular build and his height.

Gio's attention to detail extended to his accessories. A silver tie clip held the silk tie in place, and a gleaming watch adorned his wrist, a subtle nod to punctuality and precision. His cufflinks, understated yet refined, glistened as he gripped the steering wheel.

Behind the wheel, Gio merged onto the bustling streets. The engine's purr beneath him echoed the confidence that radiated from his every pore.

As he navigated the labyrinth of traffic, his sharp eyes observed the world outside his luxurious cocoon. Pedestrians became mere extras in the theater of his journey, and other drivers were inconsequential players in the grand production of his life. He reveled in the knowledge that every gaze lingered on his car, every passerby envious of the man behind the wheel.

The middle of the afternoon provided the perfect backdrop for his drive—a canvas of sunlight that illuminated the city's skyscrapers and bounced off the polished surfaces of his car. With one hand casually gripping the wheel, Gio felt the warm embrace of success in the air.

Amid the urban landscape, his mind buzzed with thoughts of triumph. He believed himself to be the best driver on these chaotic streets, maneuvering through the sea of vehicles with an unmatched skill that mirrored his legal prowess. Each turn, each calculated lane change, displayed his control over the elements.

As he passed by cafes and boutiques, he observed the city's inhabitants with an air of detached superiority. The people on the sidewalks, their lives briefly intersecting with his, were but extras in the script of his existence. He celebrated in the subtle nods of admiration from those who recognized him, a reminder that his influence extended beyond the courtroom.

Gio's thoughts, like the cityscape outside his window, were a collage of self-assurance. He mused on his courtroom victories, the accolades that adorned his office walls, and the ever-growing list of clients seeking his charismatic brand of legal representation. The city, with its towering buildings and bustling streets, was a mere stage for the grand performance that was Giuseppe Rossi's life.

He drove toward the courthouse with the poise of a man who believed the world to be his personal canvas and every moment an opportunity to assert his dominance.

He maneuvered his luxury car into a prime parking spot near the courthouse, the engine going to a satisfied halt. The city's rhythm hummed around him as he emerged from the sleek vehicle, his tailored suit and confident stride commanding attention. The courthouse loomed ahead, a bastion of justice where Gio, the orchestrator of legal theatrics, would once again take center stage.

As he approached the courthouse steps, Gio's sharp eyes caught sight of Jesse Spencer, the client whose fate now rested in his charismatic hands. Jesse, nervously pacing, looked up at Gio with a mix of apprehension and desperation.

"Mr. Rossi, I'm in deep trouble, aren't I?" Jesse's voice trembled, his eyes searching for reassurance.

Gio, his demeanor unwavering, responded with a reassuring smile. "Jesse, my friend, you're in good hands. Trust me, I've seen worse and turned it around. Just follow my lead, and we'll get through this."

Jesse fired questions in rapid succession; concern etched across his face. "What if they find out I was drunk? What if the old lady gets all the jury's favor? What if they like cats? She's a cat lady, you know. What's going to happen in there?"

Gio, ever the master of persuasion, placed a calming hand on Jesse's shoulder. "Listen, Jesse, worrying won't change a thing. I've got a plan. Just stick to it, answer when I tell you to, and let me handle the rest. We're here to make sure justice is served, my friend."

Together, they entered the courthouse, the hallowed halls of justice serving as Gio's personal stage. As they made their way through the corridors, Gio's charm extended to everyone he encountered. A nod here, a smile there—each gesture a carefully orchestrated display of his social prowess. Faces lit up as they greeted the seemingly omnipotent attorney, acknowledging his presence with a mix of respect and admiration.

Amid the legal hustle and bustle, Gio led Jesse to the courtroom, where the drama of justice would unfold. The old lady, Mrs. Candella, sat with her lawyer, the air tense with anticipation. Gio, ever the showman, guided Jesse to a strategically chosen seat, ensuring they presented a united front.

Approaching Mrs. Candella and her lawyer, Gio extended a hand with a charming smile. "Mrs. Candella, a pleasure to see you. This must be your esteemed counsel." He nodded at his competitor. "Gio Rossi, at your service."

He extended his hand towards the man whose suit was wrinkled just like his face. Gio's handshake was firm, his smile disarming, as he acknowledged the opposing legal counsel.

Mrs. Candella's lawyer reciprocated the handshake, a hint of skepticism in his eyes. "Arthur Barnes, representing Mrs. Candella. Let's hope for a fair and just proceeding, Mr. Rossi."

Gio's smile widened, a glint of confidence in his eyes. "Fairness and justice are what we're all here for, Mr. Barnes. May the truth prevail." With a courteous nod, he returned to his seat, positioning himself next to Jesse.

The courtroom became Gio's arena. He scanned the room, spotting familiar faces—judges, fellow attorneys, and court personnel. With a magnetic smile, he acknowledged each one.

The hallowed halls of justice echoed with the weight of anticipation as the honorable Judge Theodore Williams entered the courtroom, his robe billowing with gravitas. The court clerk called the case, and the proceedings began. Gio, the flamboyant showman of the legal world, stood confidently beside his client, Jesse Spencer, as the trial unfurled.

"Good afternoon, ladies and gentlemen of the jury," Gio greeted with a dazzling smile, his eyes locking onto each juror with a flirtatious twinkle. "Today, we embark on a journey of truth, and I assure you, it will be a journey you won't forget." He strolled theatrically, his tailored suit emphasizing every calculated movement.

Gio's opening statement was a masterful blend of charm and storytelling. "Now, imagine a world where appearances can be deceiving, where the complexities of human behavior dance in the shadows of misjudgment. That, dear jurors, is the world we'll explore today."

As he continued, Gio wove a narrative that painted Jesse Spencer as a character caught in the crossfire of circumstance, a victim of a series of unfortunate events. His words, like silk threads, wound around the jury, binding them to his tale of sympathy and understanding.

"But let us not be blind to the dance of deception that often accompanies such tales," Gio continued, his eyes locking onto the primarily female jurors with a hint of flirtatious enthusiasm. "In the pages of this case, you'll find a plot twist that challenges preconceived notions, a twist that reveals the true essence of justice."

His deliberate demeanor, laced with theatrical gestures, garnered nods of approval from the jury. Gio strategically flirted with the line between legal advocacy and performance art, captivating the jury with his charisma.

As the opposing lawyer began his case, Gio leaned casually against the podium, a sly smile playing on his lips. The opposing counsel presented the evidence meticulously, armed with legal jargon and a solemn demeanor. Gio, however, had a different weapon in his arsenal—the law of attraction.

"Objection, Your Honor!" Gio interjected at one point, his voice smooth as velvet. "May I remind opposing counsel that the burden of proof lies with them, and what we've seen so far barely scratches the surface. It's like presenting a puzzle with missing pieces, Your Honor."

Judge Williams, a veteran of the legal arena, raised an eyebrow but allowed the objection. Gio seized the moment, turning to the jury with a smirk. "Ladies and gentlemen, a puzzle with missing pieces is no puzzle at all. It's just a collection of disjointed fragments, each one telling a different story."

His fingers danced along the edges of the podium as he continued, his words creating a veil that obscured the damning evidence against Jesse. Gio used his wit to redirect the jury's attention, presenting the case not as a straightforward armed robbery but as a nuanced tale of human folly.

The opposing lawyer, undeterred, continued to present facts and figures, weaving a logical narrative rooted in legal precedent. Gio, however, countered with a subtle mix of humor and legal parlance, creating an atmosphere where the jury found themselves drawn to him rather than the dry legalities.

As the courtroom drama unfolded, Gio's eyes often met those of the female jurors, a flirtatious connection that transcended the boundaries of legal decorum. He strategically peppered his arguments with anecdotes, transforming the proceedings into a captivating performance that masked the absence of concrete legal strategy.

When the time for the closing statements arrived, Gio took center stage once again. "Ladies and gentlemen of the jury, today, I've shared a story with you—a story of redemption, of second chances. Now, it's your turn to write the ending. Choose justice, choose understanding, and let this tale reach its deserving conclusion."

His closing remarks resonated with an air of confidence that seemed to permeate the very fabric of the courtroom. The jury, their faces reflecting a mix of amusement and captivation, prepared to retire for deliberation.

"Court is adjourned for deliberation," Judge Williams

announced, bringing a temporary halt to the theatrics. Gio, with a nod and a wink to the jury, gracefully exited the courtroom, leaving a lingering echo of charm in his wake.

In the corridors, as the jury filed into the deliberation room, Gio leaned against a wall with a satisfied smirk. He had orchestrated a legal spectacle where charm trumped legal intricacies, and the jury, caught in the magnetic field of his persona, would soon render their verdict.

Moments blinked away as Jesse's face drenched with anxiousness while Gio calmly awaited the final call from the judge. And so it arrived, the moment of decision. Tension buzzed at the defense table and the prosecution's table as well. As the judge took his seat, the jury presented their verdict.

"We find the defendant, Jesse, not guilty!"

Relief washed over Jesse's face while Gio's lips curved into a satisfactory smile. This win was etched on his legal profile as another win, but the perils of fate stood just on the horizon, awaiting to wreak havoc in Gio's life.

Chapter 2: An Unexpected Turn

Rain pattered in the streets of Ravenbrook as dark clouds blanketed the sky. Midst the pattering of the rain outside the courtroom, Gio Rossi, dressed in a heather grey suit, paced back and forth in the hallway—the aura of nervousness emitted with each stomp of his finely polished, brown leather derby boots.

For the first time in his career, anxiousness clouded his face as his hair veiled patches of its chiseled features. Breathing out the heaviness in his heart, Gio flicked his wrists as he adjusted his tie, striving to let the confidence in him soar through the clouds of anxiousness.

The burden of the case he found himself entangled in weighed heavy on his shoulders. This was no ordinary case; it was personal. In the courtroom, his lover, Nicoletta Bianchi—an Italian woman who embodied the essence of elegance, her waves of luscious dark hair glorified her olive skin as her mesmerizing eyes hypnotized the senses of any person they met—stood trial for a crime she claimed to be innocent of. Charles Blackwood, who was previously her sugar daddy, had been murdered, drowning the small town of Ravenbrook in mysteries and horrors.

Charles Blackwood was a prominent, wealthy businessman who dwelled in the town of Ravenbrook. His physical appearance betrayed the stature he held in the business world with his extensive network of connections with other prominent people. With an intricate network of influential people across the world in his grasp, Charles rose through the ranks and made his mark.

The flame of justice burnt vibrantly in Gio's heart. When he embarked on his journey as a lawyer, he dedicated his life to defending the innocent, providing a chance to the people who have been denied the liberty of freedom through false allegations and accusations.

As Gio trod back and forth, the threads of fate of Nicoletta and his life began to entwine together. He found himself drowning in the chasm of his duty as an attorney and his unquenchable love for Nicky—hindering his senses to separate his feelings from the case. Time trickled through, and the trial was about to begin. Plagued by the unsettling emotions in his heart, Gio's consciousness wandered into the events of the past, submerging in the thoughts of how he ended up here.

Warping through the reel of memories, he arrived in the timeline of six months prior to the trial—the time when his world collided with Nicoletta's world as if guided by nature. Gio's career as an attorney was thriving. He was an esteemed attorney at a prestigious law firm, flourishing in the world of justice with his unwavering determination and sharp intellect.

He was a master at using every weapon at his disposal to win his cases. He had conquered the art of swaying the juries using his charisma and tempting looks to swirl the verdict in his favor. He marched through the courts shrouded in the aura of glamorous confidence as he was proficient in securing plea bargains and getting most of his clients off with little jail time.

Gio had made a name for himself in the realm of justice. As he delved deeper into the reel of memory, he stumbled onto the moment when he found himself defending Nicky in a minor traffic violation case.

His first meeting with Nicky had been far from orthodox. The instance his eyes drowned in her enticing gaze, invisible yet vibrant threads of connection unraveled before them, drenched in the hue of iridescent emotions, sparking a flame of the merging of two entities, the brightness of which illuminated them beyond the horizons of the courtroom.

Through the passage of months, the garden of their relationship blossomed under the breeze of adoration. Slowly, as their bond flourished, the intricacies of Nicky's personality dawned on him.

He discovered that Nicky was a woman with a captivating and charming spirit that veiled a troubled past beneath it—a past that was blanketed with heartache and loss, enchaining her heart in the hollowness of sorrows—which ignited a flicker of desire in him to protect her, to shield her from the harshness of the world.

Respect and admiration, accompanied by the emotions of love, torrented within Gio as he gazed at the woman whose each step, each action, her demeanor, her looks… Everything oozed the elixir of nobility and elegance, and yet, beneath all this, she was just a victim of a sorrowful past.

However, the fog of trials blinded their bonded path since fate has a way of testing even the strongest of bonds. The storm depicted the tales of horror to the netizens of Ravenbrook; each gust of it plagued the people's souls, and in the midst of it stood the couple, Gio and Nicoletta. Upon the whirl of the gust of the storm, the news of the murder of Charles Blackwood swirled through the town. The once vibrant bond of Gio and Nicky was now painted in the hue of anxiousness and cynicism as the prime suspect was revealed: Nicoletta Bianchi.

Ripples of doubt waved through Gio's mind as the attorney part of his mind questioned Nicky's integrity while his emotions screamed her innocence. Squirming through the evidence that painted Nicky as the prime suspect, he realized that the evidence was circumstantial but damning. Nicky had been spotted near the crime scene within the time frame of Charles's murder; the timing of her presence near the site erupted unshakable suspicions.

Shocked by the sudden revelation of the events, submerged in the turmoil of his emotions, Gio couldn't fathom the idea of Nicky as a killer. Over the past few months, every minute he spent with her, he could see the compassion and kindness Nicky emulated.

Midst the rising conflict within his entity, his mind illuminated the veiled parts of Nicky's personality—her manipulative and conniving nature. The conflict between his heart and mind became intense, forcing his quivering soul to seek the truth and unveil the mysteries of this story, this murder.

Navigating through the dust of conflictive emotions, Gio strengthened his resolve and decided to represent the woman he loved—to pour every bit of his energy into shielding her from the anguish that the world had thrown her way once again. He even resigned from his law firm to give this case his undivided focus.

The law firm was where he ascended in his career and basked in the glory of being a successful attorney, but now, he had decided to embark on a new chapter of his life, where he would power through life with Nicky by his side.

Forging his love and emotions into his resolve, Gio scrambled through the details of the investigation, analyzing every bit of the evidence meticulously. The desperation in his heart grew as he delved deeper and deeper into the intricacies of the case. He realized that beneath the haze of circumstantial evidence, dreadful secrets lurked deeper in the shadows.

Secrets that would change the course of the life they once knew.

Secrets that would unravel their lives and challenge everything they thought they knew.

As Gio realized the intricacies of the case, a fact was illuminated upon him. He couldn't use his charms and showmanship this time to dismantle the guilty verdict against Nicky, especially with Judge Enrique, the most senior and respected judge of the town, holding the reins of this case. This time, he had to arm himself with proper, legal evidence because the battlefield had changed, and now, he had to change his tactics too.

The repeated bangs erupted from the gavel, which carved Gio out of his realm of memories as he sat in his seat. The lights flickered in his eyes as his heart thumped ferociously in its cage. Nervousness formed beads of sweat in his palms as he clenched his fists. Averting his gaze from the case file before him, his eyes met Nicky's—specks of uncertainty and worry flickered in them as a faint sigh escaped her delicate lips.

Witnessing her in that state, sensing fear in her gaze, a spark of determination blazed in Gio's heart. At that moment, he decided, he promised that he would fight tooth and nail to prove her innocence even if it meant risking his entire career. He would shield her from atrocities as he once promised to himself. He would fight this battle for her sake and illuminate the truth lurking within the shadows of Ravenbrook.

Fate was penning the new chapter of their lives, of Gio's life. Little did he know that this trial was not just to prove Nicky's innocence or his legal skills but a trial of his devotion to Nicky. As the ink of fate wrote through the pages of their lives, the journey that lay ahead of them was being written with the ink of peril, danger, and the shadows of a mystery that would reveal the dark underbelly of a seemingly idyllic town.

With the flip of each page of their fate, each day of their lives, Gio would discover how far he was willing to go for love, justice, and the pursuit of the truth.

Chapter 3: Shadows of Doubt

Bangs of thunder rippled through the skies, shadowing the town of Ravenbrook. The streets were flooded with rainwater, and the courtroom resembled the tensity of the weather outside. With Nicky, drenched in anxiousness, on the stand, Gio lingered his gaze over to the jury.

His usual shenanigans of corrupting the jury by hoarding it with females, enchanting them with his charms, and swaying the decision in his favor hadn't worked in this case. Gio's consciousness warped through the simulations of trial—strategizing how he would play his cards and evidence to gain the jury's trust—the heels of his shoes stomping on the floor, erupting the echoes of his stressfulness.

"Today, we gather here to seek justice for Charles Blackwood's murder. The suspect, Nicoletta Bianchi, will stand trial for Mr. Charles's murder. The jury shall remain impartial, hear the evidence, and deliver its decision after hearing all the facts. The prosecution and the defendants shall begin by bringing the supporting evidence for their respective cases. The prosecution shall begin their case. The stage is yours, Mr. Kane."

"Thank you, your honor. The prosecution claims that the suspect, Nicoletta Bianchi, murdered Charles Blackwood in cold blood, and we have sufficient evidence and witnesses to prove it, which we will reveal in a moment," Abraham Kane, a tall man with a sleek mustache shading his upper lip, his thick dark hair combed back neatly, explained the basis of his case to the jury and the Judge Enrique as he stood from his seat. His eyes, hinting fierceness and determination, glanced at Nicky while Gio sat, judging his opponent's demeanor—finding his weaknesses and analyzing the jury.

"And what's the claim of the defendants, Mr. Giuseppe Rossi?" Judge Enrique's voice rang through the room as Gio stood up from his seat, buttoning his blazer and tightening his chest.

"Thank you, your honor. The defense claims that Miss Nicoletta Bianchi is innocent and is being framed. We have witnesses and supporting evidence which we shall bring before the jury in time," Gio's voice, brimming with confidence, soared through the room as he laid his reassuring gaze on Nicky's worried face.

"Very well. Have both the defense and the prosecution shared their witness list and evidence list with each other? Mr. Rossi? Mr. Kane?"

"Yes, your honor," both replied in unison.

"Good. I don't want unnecessary quarrels delaying the verdict, for this case holds significant importance and should be resolved soon. Mr. Kane, please begin," Judge Enrique's words of warning submerged in both lawyers' hearts as they glanced at each other – exchanging inaudible words.

"Your honor, respected jury. We have recorded proof of Mr. Charles's murder timeframe by forensics here, which is between 11 pm and 1 am. The exact same timeframe was used by a witness to find Miss Nicoletta exiting the building.

We all know Mr. Charles was a wealthy man, famous for his brilliant business mind, and a woman like Miss Nicoletta… A young, beautiful woman who has enough motive to kill Mr. Charles and inherit his insurmountable wealth."

"Objection, your honor. Improper character evidence," Gio cut off Kane's words, refraining Kane from tainting the jury's minds.

"Noted. Mr. Kane, refrain from such projections."

"Apologies, your honor. The prosecution would like to call Inspector Shirley to the stand," Kane announced as he gestured towards a young woman in her twenties dressed in her police uniform.

"Inspector Shirley, do you affirm to tell the truth, the whole truth, and nothing but the truth?"

"I do," she spoke as she raised her hand to her side.

"Inspector Shirley, would you care to explain to us what made you suspect Miss Nicoletta? I mean, there must have been something, right?" Kane stated as he strolled towards the young police officer while gesturing to the jury.

"Our department refrained from framing anyone until the evidence from the forensics had been released–"

"I'm sorry to cut you off, Inspector. Would you mind sharing your insights from the beginning?"

"Uh, sure. When we entered Mr. Charles's building, we found a trail of blood starting from the main gate all the way up to his room. Initially, we speculated that it must have been the killer's blood, but after the forensics report, that blood turned out to be of Mr. Charles. As we entered the room, we found Mr. Charles's lifeless body, butchered, as the pool of blood formed around it."

"Some heel marks, drenched in blood, were leading away from the body. When given to the experts, the shoe marks belonged to a woman in her prime of a certain weight and believed to be rich—filthy rich since the heels were of a luxurious brand that only few could afford. As we narrowed down our circle of suspects, Miss Nicoletta filled all the spots as she had been in close relationship with Mr. Charles. After the forensics report, Miss Nicoletta's DNA and fingerprints were found in Mr. Charles's bedroom, which assured us that our murderer was, indeed, Miss Nicoletta." The Inspector poured before the courtroom the analysis of the police investigation as the color faded from Nicky's face, horror swirled in her eyes. Gio sat in his chair, penning down his questions while he glanced at Nicky once in a while.

"Thank you, Inspector Shirley. Your honor, here are the results of the forensics' report identifying Miss Nicoletta's DNA presence in Mr. Charles's room, therefore, testifying to Inspector Shirley's analysis," Kane unraveled as he marched back to his desk, picked up the analysis report and gave Gio and Judge Enrique.

The look on Judge Enrique's face changed as if he had already made his decision, but Gio's unwavering resolve shone as he skimmed through its contents, formulating his plan forward.

"Will the defense cross-examine the witness, Mr. Rossi?" Judge Enrique asked, peering at Gio from above his spectacles.

Gio sat in his seat, skimming through his files and notes as his consciousness deafened towards Judge Enrique's voice. Amidst the air of anticipation and tension, Nicky's anxiousness tore through her soul as she gazed at Gio, thinking he had admitted defeat. Closing her eyes, she prepared her heart for the future that lay in front of her after she was declared guilty.

"Mr. Rossi?" Judge Enrique's voice upped, alerting Gio.

"Yes, your honor. The defense will cross-examine," Gio blurted as he gathered his files and strode towards the Inspector.

"Inspector Shirley, how old are you?" Gio inquired as he pocketed his hands, his eyes fixed on the confused Inspector.

"Objection, relevance," Kane interjected.

"Noted. Mr. Rossi, please stick to the subject."

"Miss Shirley. Is it alright if I call you Miss Shirley?" Gio asked.

"I don't mind, Mr. Rossi. Go ahead."

"Very well. Miss Shirley, I'm having trouble understanding how a twenty-four-year-old Inspector, who has just joined the force, is able to come to such a conclusion?" Gio inquired; the purpose of his question was to tamper the jury's mind by raising the question about the Inspector's credibility.

"I have just explained, Mr. Rossi. If you were listening, you wouldn't have asked such a question," specks of frustration lingered in Shirley's voice.

"That's quite a temper you have there, Miss Shirley. However, I'm finding it hard to understand how the circumstantial evidence can paint someone as a murderer," Gio continued as he glanced at the jury, judging their expressions after Miss Shirley's display of anger over a comment.

"Circumstantial evidence? Mr. Rossi, are you blind!? You just saw the analysis report by the forensics," Shirley lashed out as an expression of amusement flourished on Gio's face.

"How can I trust the judgment of someone who just lashed out over a few comments? Anyway, I have seen the report, and I'm not convinced, Miss Shirley. We all know, as Mr. Kane elaborated quite nicely, that Miss Nicoletta was in a relationship with Mr. Charles. So, it's obvious her fingerprints will be everywhere in his room," Gio continued as his voice brimmed with confidence.

A few members of the jury nodded in agreement while some whispered in each other's ears. Gio noticed his plan to plant the seed of doubt in the jury's mind had worked.

"Miss Shirley, at what time did you arrive at the scene?" Gio asked.

"At 1:30 am."

"That's an hour and a half late from the conjectured time of death. A lot of people could have barged in or out of the apartment in that timeframe, Miss Shirley."

"If the victim was murdered at 1 am, then we were only half an hour late, Mr. Rossi."

"That depends on one thing… At what time did you receive the report of the victim's death?"

"The call was…" Shirley stopped as she thought about revealing the exact time or the made-up time. She realized one thing: she had been trapped in the question.

"Answer the question, Inspector Shirley," Judge Enrique ordered.

"Uh, at 12:23 am," Shirley responded in a faint voice.

"That's an hour late, Miss Shirley. But we can assume the police were busy with other urgent matters, so that's alright. But an hour gives the culprit the time to switch the evidence, misleading the police, removing their traces, and easily make their escape, Miss Shirley," Gio announced, his words targeting the jury, sprouting the seed of doubt in their minds upon the basis of these claims.

"I ask you, Miss Shirley, if your boyfriend or husband was murdered, wouldn't the police find your DNA all over the apartment?" Gio continued, the corners of his lips curled as the jury's eyes sparkled with interest, awaiting Shirley's response.

"Objection, the defense is leading the witness, your honor," Kane raised his voice, his expression a bit grave as he noticed the ripples of confusion among the jury.

"Withdrawn. No further questions for this witness," Gio exclaimed as he marched back to his seat, embracing a smile on his face and gazing at Nicky's smiling face.

"That was good," Nicky whispered in his ears.

"I know, but we are just getting started. The prosecution's still holding a wild card. We should stay focused," Gio speculated as he squirmed his eyes through Kane's table.

"I believe in you, Gio. You are the best lawyer in my eyes," Nicky assured in a hushed voice as she blinked a smile at Gio, caressing his hand. A spark of determination lit brightly within him as he gazed at her affectionate face, her trust in him. The anxiousness that shackled their hearts began to dissipate as they found consolation in each other's warmth and trust.

After Inspector Shirley's testimony and Gio's intuitive questions discrediting the value of her words in front of the jury, the prosecution placed several witnesses on the stand, and Gio scrutinized their testimonies cleverly. Leading the witnesses into a well-laid trap of questions, he lowered the value of their words in the jury's eyes as the air around the courtroom tensed even more.

Everyone realized that more credible evidence would be needed to deliver a justifiable verdict. Judge Enrique gave the defense, Gio, three days to prepare their side of the case and prove their claim that Nicoletta was not guilty of Charles's murder.

The case that was supposed to be hurled away quickly lapsed into days stretched to months as the trial went on. Gio, alone, was fighting against a team of properly structured prosecution. The daily efforts, hitting the barriers, finding the clues proving Nicky's innocence—everything became taxing on him as his usual charming demeanor transformed into a weary look.

Gio sat in his office with his files scattered on a timber table, a glass of whiskey placed beside them as he scrambled through the evidence. His hair was disheveled, his sleeves folded, his necktie hanging loosely from his neck as his eyes strained over the contents of the short amount of evidence he had accumulated. Skimming through its contents, he crunched the paper in his fist, threw it at the door ferociously, and buried his face in his palms. Gathering his coat from the hook, he strode out of the office and marched into the dark alleys surrounding Charles Blackwood's house.

Standing in front of the house, he warped his consciousness into the mind of the murderer, trying to think through his process to find clues in it. He stood there, gazing at the house for an hour, but nothing.

The crickets chirped as the veil of night shrouded the town of Ravenbrook, instilling a tinge of eeriness in its dark, flooded streets. Strolling away from the house, Gio circled around it, trying to figure out any hidden escape route that the killer might have taken. Only a few drunkards lay asleep in the alleys surrounding the house.

The sun dawned from the eastern horizon, tearing through the veil of night as Gio wandered around the streets surrounding Charles's house. The final day of the trial was nearing as he peered at the house, the sun rising from behind it, shimmering its light around its borders and casting a shadow over him. As he loomed in the shadow, Gio contemplated the fact that he needed a crucial witness, the only key left that could exonerate Nicky from a false accusation.

As he gazed around, he realized that a two-story house stood tall in front of Charles's house, separated by the street. *'Prosecution would have already interviewed them, I guess,'* Gio thought to himself as he marched back to his office and scrambled through the evidence again.

Buried beneath the pile of files was a witness list – the first witness list that the prosecution formulated before the trial began. Squinting his eyes, Gio peered over the list as he came across the name 'Agnes McAllister.'

'McAllister, McAllister...I have seen this before,' he repeated in his mind.

'Why did the prosecution remove her from their new witness list?' He asked himself as a glimmer of hope began to shine in his weary mind. Gulping through his glass of whiskey and finishing his pasta, Gio marched outside again and ventured into Charles' house. *'The neighbor,'* he thought to himself as he tilted his head toward the neighbor's house and peered at the name board hanging by its door: 'Ken & Agnes McAllister.'

A surge of excitement and hope flushed through his heart as he rang the bell. A frail woman, her complexion pale as if blood had been sucked out of her.

"How may I help you, Mr....?" the woman spoke as her eyes gauged the man standing before her.

"Mr. Rossi. I'm looking for Miss Agnes?"

"It is her. What do you want, Mr. Rossi?" Agnes inquired bluntly.

"Madam Agnes, I hope we had met under better circumstances, but I need your assistance with something," Gio put forth speckles of hope in his words.

"If it is about the murder of Charles, you can go, Mr. Rossi. I don't have anything to say regarding it," Agnes rejected as she turned to close the door behind her.

"Miss Agnes, please! I'm the lawyer of a woman whom police are framing to save their faces. Please, I need your help. I need you to tell me what you saw that night, or else an innocent woman will be executed in this god-forsaken town," Gio pleaded as he held the door from closing with his hand.

"Justice, huh? It's quite a fancy word for this town. I'll testify, Mr. Rossi, but I have one condition," Agnes spoke as the corners of her mouth curled.

"Anything, Miss Agnes. I will comply," Gio exclaimed hurriedly.

"You have to put me on the stand and hear my testimony there. You will be in the dark as much as the prosecution. Are you willing to take this risk for *'justice,'* Mr. Rossi?" Agnes demanded as she smirked weakly at Gio.

Gio stood there, motionless as he had not imagined the nature of Agnes's request. *'It's a double-edged sword,'* he thought to himself as his expression turned grim. In the mere moment of minutes, silence lingered between the two as Gio weighed the pros and cons of Agnes's testimony. *'The prosecution removed her from the witness list, so she must know something valuable...her eyes...they are not of a deceiver. The trial is tomorrow, and my preparation is weak... I need her. It's win or lose. Without her testimony, I'll lose anyways,'* Gio thought through her offer in his mind as he stared into her eyes.

"Fine, I'll comply, Miss Agnes," Gio answered, clenching his fists as the pessimistic thoughts of things that could go wrong penetrated his heart. Imagining Nicky in the execution line drowned his heart in pits of despair as he mustered up the courage and put faith in his instincts—his lawyer instincts—which screamed in his mind that Agnes knew something crucial.

The next morning's sun rose through the skies as Gio's sleep-deprived eyes skimmed through the crucial piece of evidence he had prepared along with the line of questioning for Agnes. Grooming his weary self, he strode into the courtroom as his heart thumped with anxiousness—curiosity and uncertainty as to what awaited him and Nicky. His mind, in a state of unrest, ached with the thought that Nicky's fate was in his hands, and he wouldn't be able to forgive himself if she got executed because of him.

Sitting beside Nicky, Gio's eyes lingered over her; seeing her in handcuffs and prison uniform sent tremors of pain through his heart. Skimming his hand over her thigh, Gio spoke.

"Nicky, do you trust me?"

"I do," Nicky responded with a smile as she noticed specks of worry on Gio's face.

"Gio… You are the best thing that happened to me. No matter what they decide today. I know you tried your best, and I don't and won't regret choosing you as my attorney," Nicky poured her affection into her words as she locked her hands with Gio's.

"Thank you, Nicky," he replied, his flustered heart now an embodiment of tranquility.

The court came into session as Judge Enrique took his seat. Gio, rising from his seat, called Agnes McAllister to the stand; a wave of turmoil swirled through the prosecution's team as Kane stood up in retaliation.

"Your honor, Miss Agnes was not on the witness list," Kane blurted out.

"Your honor, I found Miss Agnes from the prosecution's

first witness list, which they, coincidentally, buried deep under the pile of documents they sent my way."

"Counsel, approach," Judge Enrique annoyingly stated as he turned the face of the microphone away.

"Mr. Rossi, I told you I don't want any disturbances like this in my trial," Judge Enrique continued agitatedly.

"Your honor, I didn't do anything wrong. Her name was on the prosecution's list, which means they had prepared for her beforehand."

"Your honor, Mr. Rossi didn't mention anything regarding any new witnesses."

"Mr. Kane, I'm in as much dark as you regarding what Miss Agnes would say. I didn't have time to prep her either."

"Mr. Kane, I'm allowing Mr. Rossi to bring the witness to the stand. You should have known if her name was on your list. I'm not responsible for your negligence," Judge Enrique said as he ordered Agnes to come to the stand.

"Miss Agnes, can you please elaborate before us what you saw on the night of Mr. Charles's murder?" Gio asked. His face was an embodiment of confidence, but his heart pounded violently as he didn't know what would come out of Miss Agnes's mouth. But he did know whatever she said would determine Nicky's fate.

"I was in my room with my husband, and we had a few guests over too that night. All of us were watching T.V. in his room when I got up from the bed to shut the drapes.

Standing by the window, I saw a woman of about 5'6" and short curly hair in a white mini skirt with golden embroidery on it, which shone as soon as she walked under the streetlight, and she was carrying a plastic bag in her hand. I was confused as I had never seen that woman in that area. But when I focused, I saw something trickling from the plastic bag, and it formed a line all the way to Mr. Charles's house's main door. Before you ask stupid questions, I realized it was blood when I saw splotches of it under the streetlamp. I screamed, and the guests we had also noticed what I saw, so you can confirm with them, too."

A wave of relief swirled through Gio's existence as he stared back at Nicky with an uncontrollable smile. Grasping hold of his emotions, Gio asked.

"Miss Agnes, thank you for such elaboration. But I'm curious, at what time did you notice all this?"

"It was around 12:15 am. I remember because we were watching the show that aired at 12:10 am, and one of the guests called it in moments later."

"Very good, thank you, Miss Agnes. No further questions, your honor," Gio's ecstatic voice soared through the room as he gazed at the jury, which was now sitting, perplexed.

"Mr. Kane, does the prosecution have any questions for the witness?" Judge Enrique asked.

"No, your honor," Kane replied through his teeth as his expression screamed the lashing his team would face after the session.

After a short recess, Mr. Kane delivered a half-hearted closing statement as he realized the blow Agnes's testimony sent to their case. But still, through the lawyer antics he learned from his seniors, he tried to cast doubt regarding Agnes's testimony in the jury's mind. Shortly after, Gio rose up from his seat, sipped through his coffee, marched in front of the jury, and began his statement.

"People, we all know that in this crooked town, framing people is nothing new. Especially if it's a woman—they are painted as greedy, lusty, bloodthirsty creatures that one is compelled to think lowly of the person being prosecuted. Nicoletta Bianchi is the same—a victim of the system, of accusations. She had enough money to live a leisurely life. She didn't need Charles's money. Her life, her fate lies in your hands, as you have seen through the hordes of evidence we all provided. Please don't send an innocent woman to the gallows—a woman who has a whole life ahead of her, her youth, her dreams."

"We all, at some point in life, make decisions that don't define us, but please, today, as we stand here, concluding the efforts of weeks, your one decision will decide if an innocent woman deserves to live or die. The prosecution hid Miss Agnes's name to keep the real killer in the shadows and frame an innocent young woman, and for what? Just so their office and the police could save face in front of the public. Today, I brought you the light of justice. I brought you the chance to illuminate this courtroom, this dark town, with the light of justice. I know you will make an impartial decision in the light of facts. Thank you!"

Gio concluded his speech as the jury listened intently. Now, the intense, mind-wrecking wait started as Gio accompanied Nicky outside the courtroom as they waited for the jury's decision.

"Thank you, Gio. I can't thank you enough, and that speech was beautiful. I hope you truly believe all that you said," Nicky, standing on her toes, whispered in Gio's ears as she gave him a nudge with a bright smile shining on her face.

"You are welcome, but let's see what the jury decides," he murmured in a low tone as he played with his fingers.

Stress and tension lingered in the hearts of everyone who stood there, especially Nicky and Gio, whose expressions of distress and weariness betrayed the smiles they put on their faces. Nicky clasped her hand in Gio's hand as she said.

"Gio, whatever they decide in there, know that I love you, and I'm indebted to you."

"Hey, I won't rest until you get a not-guilty verdict. And this, not a debt, but a mere display of my affection towards you, Nicky," Gio expressed as his eyes reflected the soul of his affection towards her.

The wait shackled their nerves and hearts as minutes turned to hours, sweat beads emerged on Gio's forehead, and Nicky's mouth began to dry in anticipation and fear. The gavel inside the courtroom banged, indicating that the jury had arrived with the verdict.

Peering into each other's eyes, finding courage in each other's warmth and trust, Gio and Nicky walked into the courtroom as the jury's representative spoke.

"In light of the evidence and the testimonies, the jury declares Miss Nicoletta Bianchi…"

Gio gulped through the rising unrest in his heart as Nicky closed her eyes, unable to bear the weight of the words that were coming out of the juror. He gazed back at Nicky and held her hand, assuring her with a head nod as the juror continued.

"Not guilty!"

Chapter 4: Unveiling Shadows

The echoes of the gavel of justice rang through the town of Ravenbrook as Nicky received a not-guilty verdict. As soon as the juror's words fell upon Gio and Nicky's ears, a wave of joy erupted from their souls, and a crescent of smiles revealed upon their faces when they embraced each other. Tears of joy trickled down Nicky's eyes as she snuggled her face into Gio's shoulder. He patted her back, instilling comfort in her overwhelmed entity.

"Thank you," Nicky whispered through her sobs.

"You're welcome," he whispered back soothingly as he wiped away her tears.

Gio gestured towards the door. "Shall we?"

"Of course, but you should tell me how you pulled this off?" Nicky demanded as curiosity sprouted within her.

"I will, but let us get to the car first, my lady," he said amusingly as he lightly bowed before her.

Midst the murmuring crowd and the hateful gazes of the prosecution team, Gio and Nicky strode out of the court. The storm had calmed down; the rain had seized to pour as the droplets trickled down from the edges of the leaves and buildings. Surrounded by the fresh aroma of the wet soil and the brisk breeze, Gio escorted Nicky towards his car.

"Okay, so where do you want me to begin?" Gio inquired as he flashed a smile at Nicky once they were inside the car.

"Where? From the beginning: How did you find that witness? How did you know she would take your side and everything," she exclaimed as she shuffled in her seat, aiming her gaze at Gio.

"Okay, sooo, let's see… At first, I did everything I could to prolong the trial. I familiarized myself with the style of the prosecution and judged the jury, what they wanted to hear, and what offended them. Every witness has a loophole, which, if you can spot, you can discredit their information. Take Shirley, for instance. She was young—a trait which, though admirable, could have some downsides, too."

"Most young ones in the force are so dissolved in the word 'justice' that everything they do seems like justice to them—which you can poke and rile them up. Shirley was confident, too trustful for their discovery that when I targeted her age and proposed that she could be wrong, she angered up, and so I used that in my favor to mold the jury's opinion of her," Gio rambled on pridefully while Nicky listened intently.

"Oh, Inspector Shirley. The prosecution should have prepped her, but it was good for us, haha. So, what's the deal with Agnes, the witness?" Nicky giggled as she poked Gio for more details.

"Miss Agnes McAllister, the cornerstone of this case. A good lawyer's trait is that he visits the origin of his case several times to find those hidden clues and theories and answer questions like what and how this could have happened. So, in my quest as a good lawyer, I surveyed

Charles's mansion several times, every nook and cranny of its surroundings, but every time, a piece remained missing from the answer I sought. I inspected the neighbors' names on their gates; there, I saw McAllister. The house's coordinates were such that most of its windows were facing the front of Charles's house."

"So, I wondered, 'How could the prosecution leave such a vital witness from their list?' I went back home and went through the horde of files that the prosecution shared with me—and after scavenging through countless files, I found an old witness list with the name Agnes McAllister on it. The missing piece of the answer I sought—it was her, and my instincts knew there was a reason the prosecution removed her from the latest list."

"Trusting my instincts, I approached her, and indeed, she was a character of mystery. I guess she was fed up with the justice system of this crooked town. Anyways, she asked if I would take a gamble in the name of justice, and I said I would," Gio narrated.

"What gamble?" Nicky inquired as curiosity drenched her eyes.

"That I hear her testimony on the stand, too. Of course, I was afraid because it was your life at risk, but something in my heart knew that it was the right choice," Gio mumbled as he lowered his eyes.

"I'm sorry that you went through all this because of me," Nicky apologized, gazing at him with affection brimming in her eyes.

"Don't apologize, Nicky. I believed in your innocence, and I promised myself that I would shield you from the shadows of this world," Gio clarified as he caressed her face.

"Who would try to frame me for this heinous crime?" Nicky pondered out loud as Gio's mind thumped with the same thought.

The question lingering in their mind was shackling every townsperson of Ravenbrook. The air of the town heavied under the weight of curiosity and skepticism—Who killed Charles Blackwood? As the news of Nicoletta's innocence spread through the town, the shadows of insecurity and fear loomed over their lives once again as their consciousness hovered over the only thought: *There was a killer among them!*

Contemplating the fact that Nicky was framed by someone to cover up their tracks and the flashes of Charles's cold body flickering through his mind, Gio's heart thirsted for the search of justice and truth. Agnes McAllister's words echoed in his mind as he winced over the fact that people's trust in justice had vanished over time.

The true essence of his profession swirled within his veins as he vowed to himself to unveil the face of the culprit before the townspeople and spark the trust in justice in their hearts once again.

"It's that lawyer, Giuseppe, something. I know he messed with the jury."

"He's suspicious, or who else could have killed Charles except his girlfriend, Nicoletta."

"I say this case was a sham. A slap in the face of justice."

"But what if she's innocent and the real killer is among us?"

"Well, then God help this hellhole of a town."

The rumors and gossip traversed through the veins of the town regarding Charles Blackwood's murder as the shadow of mystery surrounding it grew darker and darker. Some people filled up the street in front of the court, demanding a retrial of Nicoletta Bianchi. A ripple of unsettlement swept through the townspeople as, with each passing day, the fear in them began to grow. Navigating through the fog of turmoil, Gio ventured on the quest to illuminate this mystery's shadows.

"We need to flush out whoever framed you, Nicky," Gio murmured to Nicky as he hovered his gaze over the files of Charles Blackwood.

"Indeed, we do," Nicky agreed as her eyes stared at Charles's photo in a file empathetically.

"You loved him?" Gio inquired as he noticed sadness swirling in Nicky's eyes—his heart pinched.

"Not much, but he didn't deserve a death like that," Nicky sighed.

"You remember something? Something that would help us start this investigation?" Gio asked without taking his eyes off the file.

"Well, Charles... He was always in the presence of some highly influential people. However, he didn't take me along with him; he just told me how fearsome they were and that he had to keep them in check. Sometimes, I wondered what kind of business he did," Nicky blabbered on.

"We will find them, Nicky. Whoever did this, I will find them," he assured her as he hugged her.

The following morning's sun had risen through the eastern horizon as Gio, dressed in his casual attire, stepped out on the streets. As he marched towards the nearby store, he heard the murmurs of the people behind his back. Closing his eyes in response, he focused on the matter at hand as he picked up the grocery—he had planned to make breakfast for Nicky when she woke up.

Aside from his objective of preparing breakfast for Nicky, Gio had another reason for stepping out—to hear the rumors swirling around regarding Charles Blackwood.

In an hour of his time outside, all he picked up was the hatred people spewed behind his back, except for an old couple's gossip regarding a secret occult of Ravenbrook. Though interesting, Gio shunned it as it had no relevance to his person of interest. With a sigh of defeat, he marched back home and began to prepare breakfast.

Submerged in drowsiness, Nicky wobbled up to the living room as she blankly stared with a smile on her face at Gio—

his rolled sleeves, his determined gaze, his steadfast hands chopping through the onions for breakfast.

"Are you always this energetic in the morning?" Nicky chuckled as she asked Gio.

"Well, not always. Usually, I'm just too tired, so I sleep in till afternoons," he casually remarked.

"Hmmm, then what makes today special?" Nicky teasingly asked.

"Because today, I have a very special guest at my house," Gio smirked as he glanced back at her.

Nicky giggled as she rested her head on her hand and stared at his back. Sparks of affection flared through her heart as warmth spread through her veins. Shortly after, Gio laid out the breakfast before her—the aroma soaring through the piping hot dishes awakened Nicky's drowsy part of the soul as she delved into it.

Spending a pleasant afternoon together, Nicky and Gio's bond flourished as the threads of affection began to link their hearts to each other. While they relished each second of their time together, Gio's mind hovered over the intricacies of Charles's murderer while a void bellowed in Nicky's soul as the flickers of Charles's dead body flashed through her mind. The horridness of the event left the stench of a dead body etched in her soul as she couldn't carve herself out of the trauma.

The sun drowned as the darkness of the night veiled the

sky—the town's ambiance grew even more murky under the guise of night. Gio, guided by his unquenchable thirst for the truth, made his way towards the mansion of Charles Blackwood.

The opulent mansion, under the murkiness of the night and the chirps of the crickets, instilled a tinge of horror in the environment. Embracing courage, Gio trod forward as he inspected the surroundings of the house once again. With moonlight as his lamp, his eyes revolved around the minuscule details that could have aided the murderer in any way: a tall tree beside the wall, a manhole in the alley beside the mansion.

"How could the murderer have entered and not been noticed? And they were daring enough to walk out from the front door where Miss Agnes saw them," Gio conjectured as he skimmed his hand over the main gate of the mansion.

Wandering through the realms of speculations and observations he created in his mind, Gio walked into the mansion and began to search through every item his eyes lay upon. Searching through the living room, he arrived at the kitchen and skimmed through every item he could see.

Inspecting every nook and cranny of every cabinet and place he could find in the kitchen, he readied to march upstairs when his eyes caught a glimpse of the crooked crevice of the edge of a cabinet. He stepped to his side, letting moonlight seep through it. His heart skipped a beat as he slowly pulled at the crooked board of the edge.

Gio jolted in his spot as a few roaches slithered out of it. Gaining his composure back, he turned on his flashlight and buried his gaze into the hidden cabinet of Charles Blackwood. A gush of excitement traversed through his soul as he plucked out a piece of paper enveloped in a vacuumed plastic bag.

With every beat, his heart sank into the emotions of excitement and anticipation. Peeling open the bag, Gio unfolded the crisp paper in front of him—a list of initials of the names with Charles's initials, *C.B.,* penned at the top of the page.

"What the heck is this?" Gio murmured to himself as he skimmed his finger over the seal at the bottom of the page—a seal of blood.

"This is messed up. What can it be? An organization? A target list? Competitor's list? But why is Charles's name in the top-center; was he the leader?" Gio murmured to himself as his mind hovered around the facts he could conceive at the moment. His brows knitted together as he found himself standing at the brink of something perilous. He felt the death gnawing at his throat as his gaze fixated on the blood seal.

His heartbeat began to rise as he felt the intensity of the threat looming over his and Nicky's heads. Gasping for composure, Gio reined in his emotions. As he stood up, a loud creaking sound erupted from the door—suddenly, an arrow of horror pierced through his mind.

'Who is it? Is it the murderer? Have they been following

me?' A storm of thoughts gushed through his head as beads of cold sweat formed on his forehead. Hastily, he tip-toed towards the pillar near the front door. With each passing second, the thumping sound of the footsteps neared, and Gio's heart trembled with fear—and anxiety as his breath turned hefty.

'Is this the end? I haven't even begun my life with Nicky yet. I haven't fulfilled my promise to her yet. No! No! This is not the end,' Gio spun through the countless thoughts that suffocated his mind.

The footsteps came to a halt near the pillar, and Gio's heart stopped; his eyes blanked as he swung his arms towards the origin of the sound. A scream soared through the mansion as Gio's arms crashed against a person's face, making them fall onto the floor. The pent-up emotions oozed out of Gio as he yelled, jumped on top of the person, and prepared for another series of punches.

"Wait! Wait! Stop! I'm not some thief, I promise," an innocent girlish voice pleaded, carving Gio out of his rage of emotions.

"W-Who are you?" Gio stuttered as he failed to recognize the girl before him. His mind lingered over Miss Agnes' statement as she had confirmed that the culprit was a woman. Gio kept his guard up as the fear began to fade from his mind.

"I'm a journalist, Emily Turner," she explained while Gio's mind was entangled in the chains of suspicion.

His heart got lost in the haze of distrust as he clenched his fists, peering into the girl's eyes, searching for the specks of trust in them.

"I can see you still don't trust me," Emily huffed, gazing into Gio's distrustful eyes.

"This is no place for a journalist to be wandering around at this time. Of course, I'm suspicious," Gio mumbled, still refusing to let go of her.

"Okay, look, I'm here for the same reason as you. My job card is in my pocket; you can confirm it from there," Emily explained.

Hesitantly, Gio hovered his gaze around, inspecting his surroundings while he plucked out her card.

"So, you work at the Ravens News Centre?" Gio inquired, the unsettling feeling of distrust slowly dissipating into nothingness.

"Yes. Ravens News Centre…" Emily muttered annoyedly, mumbling the words of frustration under her breath.

"You people are wild, that's for sure. Always hunting for a story like hyenas," Gio poured his pent-up emotions regarding the journalists before her. A ripple of satisfaction quelled his overwhelming emotions as if a sack of burdens had been lifted off his heart.

"You are one to say. Always bleeding your clients dry like leeches," Emily retorted as she helped herself up from the ground, dusting her clothes.

Glancing at her, Gio opted to steer the conversation towards the mystery that loomed over them—hoping to gain some insight into what he might have missed.

"Clever, Miss Emily. Shall we move on then?" Gio stated as he strolled towards the staircase.

"Charles surely lived lavishly," Emily admired, submerging every bit of the mansion into her eyes.

Gio led the way toward Charles's bedroom, keeping Emily's movements in check, which prevented her from walking into the kitchen. The nooks of his lawyer mindset wanted to hide the evidence of his discovery—the list and the pried open board—until he had complete trust in her intentions.

Juggling through his scattered thoughts, he averted his gaze towards the room—splotches of dried blood splashed across the beige drapes ensnared one's attention while the rest of the room seemed to have been tidied. The walls were whitewashed, the carpets were cleaned, and the sheets were rid of blood.

"Why leave the drapes?" Gio and Emily both pondered out loud in unison.

Curiosity and a tinge of fear swirled in them both as they approached the drapes. The wind howled outside as the drapes unfurled towards them, making Emily jolt in her spot as a muffled shriek escaped her mouth. Gio skimmed his hand over the drape, burying his gaze into the hues of red and beige. With each passing second, his chest tightened with anticipation.

"Hey, Mr. Gio…W-what's this?" Emily's shaken voice squeaked through the room.

"What happened?" Gio blurted, rushing towards her.

"T-There's some logo…carved into the floorboard…and…and there's blood in it," Emily described in a hefty voice, her chest rising and falling with each breath as the nauseousness crawled up to her throat.

Arriving at the spot, Gio followed the line of her horrified yet curious gaze and aimed his eyes at the bottom of the wall beside the bed. As his eyes analyzed every bit of the sign—it was the same as the sign on the list. His mind transcended into the realms of mysteries as the threads interlinked together, unfolding a new canvas of perspective before him. Gio skimmed his index finger over the carved sign.

"The blood has dried," he uttered.

"Who could have done this?" Emily pondered as she regained her composure.

Peering into her curious, horrified, yet thirsty-for-more eyes, Gio's mind established he could trust her. This was new to her; her reactions were genuine; her eyes spoke the truth. Either that, or she's a magnificent actor. Shunning away the doubtful thoughts, he unfolded the scrunched paper from his pocket.

"What's this?" Emily inquired.

"A list I found before you arrived. Look at the bottom," Gio told her.

"The sign," Emily exclaimed.

"Yes, the sign. The way they carved this sign on the wall, too, makes it seem like it's an organization," he conjectured as he linked the scattered clues.

"Everything they have done so far... It seems so organized, so orderly, then why leave the drapes?" Gio questioned, more to himself.

"Maybe they forgot, or someone barged in while they were cleaning," Emily hypothesized while her eyes squirmed through the bottoms of every wall of the room.

"No, they seem too professional for those mishaps. They would have chosen a time when they knew they wouldn't be disturbed. They had enough time to carve the sign, after all," Gio deduced as he marched towards the window.

"Then what's your theory, Mr. Rossi?" Emily inquired, imbuing a tinge of mocking in her tone.

"My theory..." Gio mumbled; his consciousness wandered through the paradox of theories. "I believe our murderer wanted to leave this as a souvenir or some sort of sign or warning," he continued.

"Souvenir? Only the sickest of the sick minds would do that. And warning for whom?" Emily scoffed.

"Anyone who's capable of murdering is already sick, Miss Emily. Charles was involved in some—" Gio's words came to a halt as he stared silently into the darkness of the night.

"Involved in what?" Emily asked, but only silence echoed in response. Tilting her head, she lay her eyes on Gio's stiff body, his eyes glaring into the shadows on the street. "Mr. Rossi, are you alright?" She checked as she poked Gio on the arm.

"Did you see that, Miss Emily? I felt it. Someone was staring at me from across the street," Gio whispered as he refused to take his eyes off the street.

"Who was it!? Did you see their face?" Emily questioned energetically.

"No, it was too dark, and they were wearing dark clothes and had masked their face. But those eyes… They were… Beast-like. Cold. Emotionless. Frightening," Gio elaborated.

Part of his soul relished the fact that it was a matter of time before he unveiled the face of the person behind that mask—who was it? Who could it be? The questions of mystery flamed the intrigue in his heart, but the claws of fear tore through him as he remembered Nicky. If he had been noticed, then she was in danger, too. The thought of it sent shivers down his spine.

"Miss Emily... May I just call you Emily?"

"Yes, of course."

"Very well. You may call me Gio. Emily, let's meet at the coffee shop near Jerrett Street at 3 p.m. It's getting late,"

Gio said as he made his way toward the main gate.

"O-Okay," Emily stuttered, baffled by Gio's sudden flip in the mood.

"Do you live nearby? I'll drop you home first," Gio offered once they were out of the house.

"Yeah, it's just right around the corner. I'll walk. Thanks, see you in the afternoon," Emily smiled as she waved him goodbye.

Worries stormed through Gio's heart; with each step, Nicky's face and those cold-blooded eyes flashed through his mind as he hurriedly made his way toward his house. Under the moonlight and the blanket of the night, a pair of sleek eyes hovered over his existence from a height—as Gio vanished into a corner, so did the eyes behind a curtain.

Gio was entangled in a web of restlessness for the whole night; his mind scrutinized the theories of this maze against the clues he had found. Midst his restlessness, shuffling in his bed, he gazed over at Nicky sleeping on the side—just the sight of her sent ripples of comfort through his anxious heart. Time sneaked through the rift of distress as the morning dissuaded the murkiness of the night.

"You look as if you have an unwinnable case today, Gio," Nicky commented as she sipped through her coffee.

"It's nothing. Just the lack of sleep," Gio mumbled as he absorbed himself into the newspaper regarding Charles's associates and their views regarding his murder.

"This murder got you occupied, huh?" Nicky whispered from behind his ear as she leaned over the sofa.

"Did you know any of them?" Gio inquired, pointing at the men and women in the paper.

"Some," Nicky answered bluntly.

"You think you can get us in a room with them?" Gio questioned, hoping he could see this box of paradox from another perspective.

"I can, but who's we?" Nicky interrogated playfully, pinching his cheeks.

"It's just this reporter I met, Emily Turner. She works for the Raven News. You can come along too," Gio explained with a weak smile.

"Of course, I'll come. Besides, this meeting won't be possible any other way," Nicky clarified as she jumped onto the sofa beside Gio.

"Why not? Don't tell me you are involved with these people, Nicky," Gio said worriedly, peering into her eyes.

"No, no, these people… Charles introduced me to them, and we were on good terms. I guess this bunch was not the one he was afraid of," Nicky assumed as she weakly smiled at Gio.

"Can I tell you how happy it makes me to see you safe?" Gio mentioned as he poked his nose against hers.

"You can…" Nicky mumbled as Gio's warm breath

scattered across her face. Giggling, she pulled back and stood up. "If we need to meet them by 3, then I got to make some calls," she said, winking at Gio.

"Very well, I shall oblige, my lady," Gio chuckled along.

The clock ticked relentlessly as Nicky indulged herself in the phone calls while Gio relished the moments of peace, readying himself for the interviews ahead. Soon, the clock hit 2:30 p.m., and they were on their way to the coffee shop near Jerrett Street. Gio's lustrous car hummed through the narrow streets of the town, turning the heads of the passersby as the clouds foretold the coming of another storm. Stepping out of the car, Gio and Nicky walked towards the shop in each other's embrace, and the people eyed them with hatred and disdain.

"Ignore them. They are just sour that they couldn't get a girl like you," Gio commented, smirking at her while his heart thrummed with uncertainty—uncertain of the presence of the organization.

"You know well, Gio, why they are acting like that. To them, I'm still a killer," Nicky's weak voice shackled Gio's heart in empathy as he immediately embraced her.

"Let them believe whatever they want. I'm here for you, and I know you are innocent, Nicky. People are scared, and fear makes the best of people irrational," Gio whispered as he patted her head.

"Thank you, Gio," Nicky murmured as she kissed his cheek and stepped back. A vibrant smile glowed on her face as she sank her eyes into his.

"Shall we march inside then, my lady?" Gio imitated the royal accent as he slightly bowed before her.

Taking Gio's hand, Nicky walked alongside him into the coffee shop. In the corner of the shop, the eyes of the girl shone up as she hurriedly signaled them to join her.

"This is Emily Turner. Emily, this is Nicoletta," Gio introduced them as he sat beside the window.

"I know. I have been heartily involved in your trial since the start. I'm glad you got the not-guilty verdict because I could see that the prosecution was hiding something," Emily rambled on.

"Ah, thank you," Nicky expressed her gratitude with a smile—a tinge of comfort swept through her heart upon seeing Emily's belief in her innocence, unlike others.

"Apparently, Emily's quite a chatterbox," Gio joked from the side, making light of the mood.

"See yourself in the courtroom," Emily retorted.

"Alright, alright, they'll be here soon," Nicky shushed them both as she averted her eyes to the door.

"Who? Who'll be here soon?" Emily inquired with a puzzled look.

"Ah, Charles Blackwood's associates," Gio answered.

"You mean the—"

"Yes, the ones who were interviewed recently," Gio cut

her off before she revealed any further details before Nicky.

He had planned to disclose the details to Nicky when he had some answer instead of simply adding to her worries. From the side, he signaled Emily to silence.

"O-Oh, they are a wild batch, haha," Emily acted along.

"Apparently, they were close enough with Charles to know about his business deals," Nicky revealed.

"Business deals? The newspaper said that there was some power struggle ongoing in the company, but it started after Charles's murder," Gio added.

"That's what the news says, or they say. It's no different. You know well they have every news station in their pockets. If you bring one such story against them, the news bans you for months," Emily complained with a sour face.

The bells of the coffee shop chimed as three figures—a tall, burly man with slicked-back hair and a cigarette in his mouth, an older man with a scar across his lips that were holding a cigar, and a woman dressed in a luxuriously crafted suit—walked in.

"They are here. The three disciples of Charles, or as he referred to them," Nicky said as seriousness swarmed her face.

"Weren't there five?" Gio inquired.

"There are. The other two... Well, let's see how it goes with them first," Nicky declared, playing with her fingers as anxiousness knitted her brows together.

The air on the table turned heavy as the tapping sound of the heels of the gentlemen and the woman's shoes and heels neared them.

Chapter 5: The Whispers in Twilight

The ticking of the clock, the clinking of the spoon, the murmurs of the people in the coffee shop—every sound was muffled in Nicky's consciousness. Only the anxiousness remained.

Fear.

Uncertainty.

Her heartbeat began to rise as the trio neared them. Clenching her fists, mustering up the courage, and putting on the veil of a smile, Nicky elevated from her spot. As she gasped to utter her words, she felt a gentle touch on her back.

It was Gio.

A comforting sensation trickled down her soul while Gio shone an affectionate smile at her.

"I'm glad you all could come," Gio greeted. "Gentlemen. Lady," he continued, gesturing for each to take a seat.

"You must be Giuseppe Rossi—the infamous lawyer: the hero of Nicoletta and a villain for the townspeople," the older man asserted, speaking through his cigar.

"A keen judgment, Mr. Vince," Gio muttered, feigning a smile while they all settled down.

"Giuseppe, Emily. Vince, Fredrica, Milton. Everyone, this is Giuseppe and Emily," Nicky chimed in, introducing everyone while she guided the guests to their seats.

"Thank you, Miss Nicoletta. A sweetheart as usual," Milton—the tall, burly man whispered, aiming a lustful gaze at Nicky while he puffed out a ball of smoke.

Fanning away the smoke with her hand, Nicky settled in her seat. In the embrace of Gio, a sense of security swarmed her as her usual elegant demeanor surged back. Time drizzled away as the group immersed themselves in the pleasant conversation while Gio and Emily focused on laying the groundwork for their interview.

"Nowadays, you don't even know what to believe and what not," Gio added as he twisted the fettuccine around his fork.

"What do you mean, Mr. Rossi?" Fredrica questioned, slicing through her steak—her eyes stuck on the core of the meat.

"I mean—"

"I think what Gio meant to say is most of the assets of this town are open for bidding. News or courts. Whatever," Emily interjected, hovering her gaze through the trio sitting in front of her.

"Well, that's quite sharp, Miss Emilia," Vince noted as he ran a toothpick through his teeth.

"Emily."

"I apologize. I reckon age is catching up to me," Vince chuckled faintly, cutting off his cigar.

"The one thing money can't buy, old man," Milton joked

from the side while Vince grunted.

"Amusing, Milton. Now, let's get to the point. Nicoletta, I'm sure you didn't invite us here for mere chit-chat," Fredrica intervened as she bore her gaze into Nicky.

With a flick of her wrist, Nicky picked up her glass of champagne. Flourishing her gaze with the marrow of confidence, she peered into Fredrica's eyes and spoke.

"Charles's murder."

"Ah, did we not send our condolences, Vince?" Milton sneered from the side.

"I believe we handed them to you," Vince growled.

"Gentlemen. It's not about your condolences. You gave this interview after his death. And you mentioned some power struggle," Gio explained. "Everything seemed so peaceful with them."

"It was peaceful. As we mentioned, it started after his death. The seat at the top was empty, and there were many who sought that," Fredrica elaborated nonchalantly.

"Who got the top seat then?" Nicky inquired.

"Me, Miss Nicoletta. As you know, I was Charles's favorite. So, it was natural it got to me," Vince answered, glaring into Nicky's eyes.

"How did you do it, Mr. Vince? I believe you must have faced some retaliation. Since you said it was a *power struggle*," Emily questioned, while her tone brimmed with journalistic essence.

"Vince didn't step up at first. That's why there was a struggle. Once he did, everyone acknowledged him as Charles's successor," Milton kneaded the story further.

Doubt flickered in Gio's eyes as he orbited his eyes around the trio's face—behind the veil of confidence and pleasant smiles, some sinister secret lurked. His instincts throbbed with curiosity.

"Mr. Milton, if you don't mind my asking. Who could have murdered Charles? As far as we know, there couldn't have been any other reason to off him like that," Gio poured his thoughts before them. His eyes fixated on their faces, searching for the truth in their expressions. "Except for one. Power. Hold of the company," he continued.

Fredrica's eyebrows flinched as she puffed out empty air while bobbing her head.

"Careful, Mr. Rossi. You might be aiming your insinuations at the wrong person," Fredrica warned.

"Insinuation? Come now, Miss Fredrica. We didn't call you here to insinuate you of such a heinous crime. We just want to know the truth, and who better to understand it from than people like you—Charles's closest associates. Nicky deserves that at least," Gio retorted as he sat cross-legged across from Fredrica.

"We ourselves have only seen the glimpse of truth, Mr. Rossi," Vince mumbled in a low voice, flicking the embers of his cigar into the tray.

"That glimpse might illuminate our whole vision, Mr. Vince," Gio persuaded with a smirk.

"Listen, son. Some might say that Charles had it coming. The businesses he was involved in were contaminated with death. Illegality. The people he had expanded his circle to, they don't play around," Vince elaborated in a grave voice. Coldness dispersed through his gaze.

"What businesses? What people?" Emily intervened, her heart ecstatic as she could see the glimpse.

"Business on the other side of the horizon of the legal system. Every nature of it. While the people he involved himself with... They hold the reins to decide the fate of anyone in this town, Miss Emily," Milton further explained. A tinge of fear crawled through Emily's spine as she felt the weight of Milton's words.

"I guess that's why he kept me out of that life," Nicky whispered.

"Charles adored you, Miss Nicoletta. Our condolences for his early departure," Vince said humbly. "To Charles," he raised his glass of wine.

"To Charles," everyone uttered in unison. As the glasses clashed against each other—it seemed in that clinking sound, everyone's true nature had been poured in. Once again, behind those elegant words, Gio's mind perceived something—the feeling of that shadowy figure from last night.

"We had warned Charles of the various threats rising from his circle, but he discarded it like any other suggestion we had," Fredrica muttered as she gulped through her wine, the muscles of her face twitching.

At that moment, Vince's face turned sour, as if Fredrica had shared more than he had expected. Picking up a scrap of clues that spilled before him, Gio glanced at Emily—hinting her to squeeze more details out of her.

"What kind of threats? Was it regarding his position at the top?" Emily baited.

"Threats, you know. Life threats, I guess," Fredrica tried to steer the conversation away once she felt Vince's discomfort with her revelation.

"Mr. Milton, were these threats regarding the usurpation?" Gio pitched the question to Milton, trying to catch him off guard.

Words betrayed Milton as he gasped for them, his eyes ricocheting from one place to another in confusion.

"I believe we should end this meeting while everything's still intact," Vince projected as he stood up from his seat. Following his lead, Fredrica and Milton stood up, too—sweat glistened on their foreheads.

"Very well. It was a pleasure meeting you all," Gio said with a bow.

"Thank you for your time, Mr. Vince, Fredrica, Milton. I hope you bring Miss Alessia and Mr. Wagner with you next time," Nicky said, feigning a smile at them.

"Alessia and Wagner, huh? I can't promise you, Nicoletta. Those two are busy souls, but I'll try," Vince chuckled as he waved his hand and strode out of the coffee shop.

With the departure of the guests, the fog of stress dispersed as they slammed down into their seats, pondering over the fragments of clues they gathered. The chains of doubt shackled Gio's mind as it kept hovering over that feeling—the eeriness he felt resonated with the same feeling of that night.

On his side, Emily compared the pieces of clues to the segment of information she had gathered during her solo investigation while Nicky contemplated the role of Alessia and Wagner.

Today's meeting sowed the seed of doubt in her heart for the associates, but suffocating darkness clawed at her, thinking about the duo that wasn't present today. She had heard nothing but sinister things from Charles about them.

"I think we all know by now that there's something more going on," Gio broke the silence.

"They know more than they were saying," Nicky conjectured.

"Either they were a part of this murder, or they know who

did it," Emily said, burying her gaze into her journal before her.

With each passing minute, the sun drowned in the west, marking the beginning of dusk as Gio, Nicky, and Emily made their way back home. Emily had hitched a ride with them. Tearing through the enigmatic cloud of dust, Gio's car revved through the streets while the figure disguised in shadows flashed in his eyes. Dropping Nicky off at the house, Gio made his way to Emily's house.

"I was thinking we should nose around the neighborhood. Confirm our suspicions about Vince and others' involvement. We know their faces now; someone might remember," Gio put forth his idea.

The moment the last word left his mouth, he squinted his eyes as a deafening sound of the horn reverberated in his ears while bright headlights blinded his eyes. Fear. Death. His soul shrieked while his mouth gasped at the scene unfolding before him.

"Hey! Hey!! Gio! Are you alright?" Emily's voice carved him out of his trance—beads of sweat dripped down from his chin while horror reflected in his eyes.

"A-Are we alive?" He stuttered.

"What do you mean? You just drove us off the road. Thank God I applied brakes on time, or we would have been crushed between the roof and the road," Emily huffed as she peered into Gio's eyes worriedly.

"B-But there was this…these headlights, and honking. It was coming at us," Gio mumbled as he tried to piece together his thoughts—his memories.

"There was nothing like that. Maybe you fell asleep, Gio. We should probably do this another day. You should go rest."

"No, no, I'm fine. We need to cover this and find more details before they cover any more of their tracks," Gio insisted as he sprinkled water over his face from the bottle.

"Are you sure?"

"I'm sure of the fact that there is something sinister slithering in the shadows of this town, and I'll uncover it before any more innocent get framed for their deeds," Gio muttered, gritting his teeth while the flame of resolve burned in his eyes.

Midst the murkiness of the dying sun and the creeping shadows of the alleys of Ravenbrook, Gio and Emily trod forward, analyzing the people whose path cojoins with Charles Blackwood's mansion. Minutes continued to pile up as they still waited to witness one soul wandering around there. Impatience surged within both. *'Were they too late?'* a single thought crossed their minds when, from behind a bunch of stray dogs, Gio sighted a rare breed.

"Emily, does that dog look like a stray to you?" Gio inquired, tiptoeing to keep it in sight.

"Seems like someone forgot to chain it tonight," Emily

pointed out while she scattered her gaze around the streets, looking for any passerby.

"It's going somewhere," Gio said, eyeing the dog.

"Probably home, Gio. Focus on the task," Emily sighed.

Minutes turned to hours. The patience of the duo was about to fade away into nothingness when a thin figure strolled down the street under the flickering streetlight. Hope ignited in the duo's heart as they both approached the thin man.

"Mister, we think you could help us with something," Emily said, her tone pleading.

"At this hour? What is it?" The man spoke—his voice frail and weak.

"Yes, um, do you live around here?" Gio pitched in.

"Yes, I do. Why? Your questions seem too personal, young'uns. Why do you ask?" Specks of agitation cultivated on the man's face.

"We wanted to inquire if you had seen someone around Mr. Charles's house around the time of his murder," Gio continued.

As if silence had devoured every bit of energy from the man's body—his face turned pale as he, in haste, strode forward on his path. Confusion tackled Gio and Emily's consciousness as they chased after the man.

"Excuse me, sir. What happened?" Emily yelled from

behind.

"You people will bring death upon us all. Woe on you," the man spat on Gio's shoes as his body shivered with anger and frustration.

"What…just…I don't get it. Death? And a civilian knows it?" Emily pondered as confusion and fear flogged her resolve.

"This runs deep. Remember how everyone began to revolt against us after Nicky's trial? I figured that they knew of the party responsible for this," Gio speculated as his eyes tore a hole through the back of the frail man.

"Let us ask someone else," Emily said as Gio's words revolved around in her head, poking the faded memory—a memory that had shaped her life but scarred her soul for eternity.

Complying with Emily's idea, Gio walked along and stood by the alley. The flashes of that shadowy figure squirmed through his mind as the cackles began to echo. Realizing that he stood at the brink of the world of reality and hallucination, he slapped his face as he pinched his thumb to awaken himself. Emily, from the corner of her eye, noticed his discomfort but feigned ignorance so as not to add further to it.

The hours of the morning were nearing, and they could only find three more passersby in the area. As if a curse had bound their tongues, words betrayed every single soul once Charles Blackwood's name fell upon their ears. The enigma surrounding this mystery grew deeper and deeper as, under the weight of this burden, Gio's mental health deteriorated with the thoughts of the shadow of death lurking in his shadows.

As the first ray of morning pierced through the veils of night, Gio and Emily understood one thing—the further they dive into this, the more they can feel the claws of death tightening around their necks. Gio, though struggling with the hallucinations, mustered up the will as he promised to dig up the skeletons these people were trying so hard to bury—the secrets of this accursed town.

Chapter 6: The Eclipse of Revelations

The scroll of events unfurled in Gio's mind. Each page represented a piece of memory, from the burdens of trial to the wretched mysteries of Ravenbrook and its residents to the mysterious stalker. The anima of his mental strain dispersed upon his face as, amidst his sleep, he winced. Was it fear? Tiredness? His soul shuddered in the realms of uncertainty as suddenly, jolting, he woke up. His breath was hefty, his eyes wobbly, and his body sweaty.

"Gio! Are you alright!?" Nicky's worried voice lay upon his ears as he felt the warmth of her hand on his head.

"I-I'm fine. Just a nightmare," Gio said, steering away from the conversation. His heart couldn't muster up the courage to lay this burden of his investigations, these paradoxical events on Nicky. As he caressed her face with his gaze, he reassured himself that it was his responsibility to keep her safe. To not let her be a tool of any other conspiracy.

"You have a fever," Nicky said. Minutes trickled through as Nicky stared at Gio's face, lining her thoughts as she read the worrisome scripts in Gio's eyes. "You can talk to me, Gio. I know I have been struggling with my own thoughts lately, but I don't want my troubles to be a wall between us," Nicky poured her thoughts into words.

"I know you have been investigating everything on your

own. You barely come home. You barely rest. You are shouldering all this stress along for my sake. I know. But it makes me feel guilty, Gio. I feel like I am the reason for it. So, please, let me be a part of this, and know that you are not alone in this fight," she continued; a bead of tear drizzled down from her eyes as she clasped her lips to seal her overwhelming emotions.

A ripple of guilt swept through Gio's soul as he embraced her in a hug. "I didn't know you felt this way. I thought if I shouldered it alone, you wouldn't have anything to worry about," he explained as he snugged his face into her shoulder. Their heartbeats synchronized amidst the storm of emotions, their souls united under the shade of serenity.

Heaving out a sigh of relief, Gio fell back into his bed as Nicky placed a cold patch on his forehead and snuggled into his arms.

The morning sun soared into the sky, marking the beginning of the afternoon, as Gio finished his and Emily's progress in investigations. The list. The mysterious stalker. The blood-smeared curtains. The murkiness around Charles's mansion. The silent and fearful neighbors. The doubts regarding Charles's associates and their involvement. Everything skewed into his words, Gio presented before Nicky as she listened intently. For a moment, Gio's mind stumbled upon Nicky's fearless expression. Fearless and determined.

A spark of courage and affection inspired in Gio's heart. Witnessing Nicky's unwavering resolve, Gio decided to confide in her and scattered his scrambled thoughts, suspicions, and theories before her.

"This is a Pandora's box. But I don't understand why people don't cooperate. I mean, isn't it to their benefit if this monstrous power was uprooted?" Nicky pondered out loud.

"Power, Nicky. Fear of unattainable, untouchable, unreachable power. It's in human instinct to fear what they can't perceive for themselves. Whoever our culprit is, they sure know how to manipulate the minds of people," Gio revealed his thoughts as he jumped up from bed and poured himself a glass of milk.

Immersing herself in Gio's words, Nicky stared at the ceiling for a minute before she jumped up and joined Gio at the kitchen counter.

"So, what's our next plan?" She asked as she hugged him from behind.

"We need to break someone from this town. We need more information, and these people certainly know something juicy," Gio explained as he chugged on the milk.

"Well, that makes sense. Should I come along?"

"Where? To stalk and interview people? Are you sure you want that, Nicky?" Gio asked, raising his eyebrow skeptically.

"Why? What's wrong with me? Emily can do it, and I can't?" Nicky pouted.

"Come now, you know it's not like that. That is Emily's

job. She's trained for that. You know I can't put you at risk again. These people have already targeted you once indirectly," Gio said, holding her hands as he gazed into her eyes.

"Fine. You always had a way with your words," Nicky mumbled as she marched into her bedroom.

Chuckling in his spot, Gio ate through his toast and contacted Emily. They decided to meet up in the pub down Thymes Street—the street upon which Charles's mansion is located.

Time sifted through the rift of anticipation as Gio, dressed in his masterfully stitched coffee brown suit and sparkling dark brown leather shoes. As he walked into the pub, a luxurious scent trailed behind him from his branded perfume. A few eyes turned as they watched him stride towards a girl settled on a table in one corner.

"Woah! What's with these nobility vibes?" Emily joked, giggling under her breath.

"Don't be stupid. A gentleman is defined by his etiquettes and dressing—a neatly cut and stitched suit from a master cutter," Gio retorted as a proud smile flashed across his face, revealing his teeth.

"Oof! Too bright! I'm blind," Emily laughed, relishing the annoyed yet embarrassed expression on Gio's face. "I'm sorry, I'm sorry; I guess I just had a couple of extra drinks," she continued.

"Tasteless. Alright, tell me why we are here and not in Charles's neighborhood?" Gio inquired as he settled down in his seat.

"Because that place is dry. This place is juicy," Emily squeaked, poking her finger to her temple, indicating her intelligence.

"What do you mean, big brains?"

"I mean, a pub is a place where people gossip. This place encourages weakness. And weak people break easy," Emily explained.

"Let's hope your wisdom applies here," Gio muttered as he hovered his gaze around.

The murmurs and cheers of the customers vibrated through the pub. The clanking of dishes, the rising smoke from the nearby barbeque grill, the jizz of overflowing beer, the dim lighting—an ambiance of joy was set, yet beneath this veil of joy lay an abyss. Gio realized that as he pointed his hearing to the nearby tables, his eyes squirmed through the customers, searching for a suspicious presence.

Meanwhile, Emily strode towards suspicious-looking people and chugging through her beer; she began to use her feministic charms to carve out details from them. Minutes passed by, as minutes turned to hours, and the hour of dusk was nearing. Patience ran thin in the duo, but the resolve stayed unwavering.

As the clock struck the hour of 5, the bells of the pub's

door chimed as two men, dressed in casual attire, but their eyes—hungry, fearful, anxious—caught Gio's attention. Processing their expressions through his legal mind, Gio remembered those eyes—the eyes of someone who was hiding something and didn't want people to know.

Hastily, Gio tapped Emily's shoulder, alerting her of the situation, and strode towards the nearby table. Masking himself in a batch of drunkards, Gio began to eavesdrop on their conversation as they joined another gentleman at the counter.

"Just make sure everything's set for the old mill," one of the men muttered, a sense of urgency lacing his words. "It's got to go smoothly, no hiccups, or else it'll be our heads next."

"Next? Old mill?" Gio wondered if they talked about Charles. "Did you get that?" He whispered to Emily.

"Yeah. The old mill. There are two of them. But when are they meeting? What is there?" Emily continued the train of thought.

After a few drinks, the gentlemen left as Gio, grabbing Emily's hand, squirmed through the crowd, following them. As soon as he barged open the door, only dust blew on the streets as no sign of life was in sight. Bewildered yet stricken with suspense, Gio aimed his eyes at Emily.

"We need information about that meeting as soon as possible. I figure that's where all our answers lie," breathed Gio, patting Emily's shoulder.

"Let's start with questioning people," Emily suggested.

"People? Didn't we try that?" Gio said.

"We did, but not with the old residents. These three spots are the hub of information, and if they don't know, then there's a chance no one in this town will know. And this meeting sounds like a cult—an old cult, and the owners of these three places are the oldest ones in town. Surely, they will know of something as wicked as this," Emily elaborated her plan. Specks of pride scattered over her face.

"Which three spots? I guess one of them would be The Little Bakery of Old Lady Martha, but what are the other two?" Gio asked.

"Old man Jenkins, the Postman, and the librarian, Diana."

"Clever. Let's get on with it then."

Igniting the embers of confidence in their hearts, they breathed in confidence and drove to their first spot—The Little Bakery.

With courage and determination guiding their footsteps, Gio and Emily strode into the bakery—stepping into the warm, inviting, aroma-filled space—a place that seemed untouched by the filthiness and darkness of the accursed town of Ravenbrook. An old lady, with her eyes sunken yet buried in the cake before her, elegantly crafted its shape and embellished it with miniature embossing of chocolate. A tremor of hunger growled through Emily's stomach.

"Excuse me, is Miss Martha here?" Gio inquired, tapping

his ring on the countertop.

"What do you require, young man? Can't you see I'm busy," the frail old voice shivered in the air.

"I see that, and I apologize for the intrusion, Ma'am. But the matter is of urgency, and it can't wait," Gio pushed.

"There's always time for a delicate dessert, child. Take a seat; your friend looks famished," Martha smiled as she plucked a slice of cheesecake and some panna cotta on the side.

"Let's just have a bite," Emily whispered as her eyes fixated on the plate.

Moments later

"So, tell me, what is it you want to know from these old bones?" Martha muttered.

"Do you know of Charles Blackwood and his recent murder?" Gio inquired, his eyes studying the face of the old lady.

Without flinching, the old lady sat in her spot with her eyes closed. "I do," she sighed.

"Apparently, he was involved in something wicked. Do you perhaps know of an old mill or any old cult that thrived in Ravenbrook?" Gio leaned in, whispering to not alert any customers.

"Child, though your purpose seems pure, there are some things that should be left unadded, or you might poison the entire dish," Martha muttered as she rose up from her seat.

"What do you mean?" Emily chimed in.

"It means the path you walk—one misstep and death will haunt Ravenbrook," Martha warned, her frail hands trembling behind her back.

"What about the mill? Where is it?" Gio yelled in a hushed tone as Martha walked away.

"Good day, you both. I hope you come again to enjoy my desserts," she spoke, waving her hand.

The shade of disappointment loomed over Gio's face as he clenched his fists—the warning of Martha lingering over his neck as a cleaver, but with courage, he strode towards his car, and Emily followed.

"Who's next?" Gio sighed.

"Old man Jenkins," Emily responded while her eyes inspected the frustration on Gio's face.

"Hey, we will figure it out, you know. Even though Martha was reluctant, we still got an assurance that Charles was part of some evil cult. Let's just figure it out piece by piece," Emily assured Gio.

"I know, but the longer this goes on, I fear Nicky will be faced with danger...again," Gio mumbled as his eyes reflected his worry for Nicky.

"She won't. I have seen it in her eyes, Gio. She's more than capable of taking care of herself. The way she glared into Vince's eyes, I knew she was no ordinary woman. Besides, that stalker seems to be after you—the one nosing around."

"Haha, thanks, Emily. That was comforting now," Gio chuckled as the vehicle revved through the streets towards Jenkins's house.

Under the flickering light of his living room, Old Man Jenkins recounted tales of Ravenbrook that seemed to blur the lines between fact and folklore. But when the conversation veered towards Charles Blackwood and the events surrounding the murder, his storytelling came to an abrupt halt.

"Young folks should be careful digging into matters that don't concern them," he warned, a tremor of fear in his voice. "Some secrets are buried for a reason. Disturb them, and you might not like what you find."

"Unfortunately, we must excavate this truth that's been haunting this town for ages, Jenkins," Gio said, his voice solidified with strength and courage.

Jenkins's eyes, filled with the weight of unspoken knowledge, conveyed a message clearer than words ever could: some truths were better left undiscovered. But seeing the embers of resolve in Gio's eyes, he sighed. "Find your way to the library and sift through the books in the eastern corner of the room. Tell Diana to guide you to the compartment where the axis collides and a rift forms. There, if you have the heart to bear it, you will find truth within the pages."

The complexion of hope blanketed their faces as Gio and Emily's eyes lit up. Thanking Jenkins for his help, they made their way to the library—an old building, its top reaching the skies while its base veiled behind the trees. Its structure was rusted and weathered.

Arriving at their destination, Gio and Emily made their way into the library, arming themselves with the weapon of caution and anticipation; they ventured through the narrow halls amidst the dancing flames of candles.

"Well, this is spooky," Emily said.

"Tell me about it. A befitting place for the secret it holds," Gio responded as he aimed his gaze at the oil paintings on the wall.

Approaching the woman dressed in the old vintage dress, sitting behind her desk, reading a book, Gio and Emily introduced themselves. Diana lifted her eyes, judging the visitors, and delved back into her book.

"We-"

"You don't seem to be here for books but tainting this den of knowledge with your impure problems. Get out before I call the authorities," she warned without taking her eyes off the book.

"The temper," Emily whispered under her breath to Gio.

"To be fair, Diana, we come seeking knowledge. Word has it in town that you are the person to go to for such purposes," Gio persuaded, pulling out his charming demeanor.

"Your eyes tell something else, young man. Don't make a fool out of me," Diana retorted.

"We come seeking knowledge of the history of Ravenbrook. The cult…The organization that had Charles murdered," Gio revealed.

Diana, always a bastion of knowledge, seemed uncharacteristically hesitant as Gio and Emily presented their inquiries. Her usual enthusiasm for research and history vanished, replaced by a guarded caution.

"Ravenbrook is a place of many layers," Diana admitted, her fingers nervously tracing the edge of an ancient tome. "But not all stories are meant to be told. Some chapters are better left unturned."

Her reluctance was a testament to the pervasive fear that had taken root in the heart of Ravenbrook—a community entangled in its own web of mysteries and secrets.

"We are here to unravel those layers, Diana. This town has been shackled far too long. People have the right to live without the claws of death tightened around their necks," Emily added from the side.

"I was once like you, young lady. The aspirer of truth. But the truth, sometimes, is harsh. Inevitable. You see a glimpse of it; you lose a limb. You unveil it further; you lose the reason to live," Diana rambled on, her eyes filled with regret as if they were hovering in the streets of the past.

"Someone has to do it," Gio added as he leaned forward. "Please guide us to the spot where the axis collides, and the rift opens."

Diana jolted in her spot—her face a canvas of emotions. But the look in Gio and Emily's eyes reassured her heart.

"It's been long since someone repeated those words. Come with me," Diana sighed as a weak smile played on her face.

In the corner of the library hall, Diana marched. Skimming her hand over a cabinet, she shoved open a hidden room—clouds of dust suffocated them as they coughed. The room was brimming with books—their leather bindings told they held the information from decades or maybe even centuries ago.

A wisp of excitement, yet reluctance roped Gio's heart. Standing on the brink of answers, Gio readied himself and began to skim through the horde of books.

While rummaging through a stack of old newspapers and letters in the local library's hidden archive, Emily stumbled upon an unmarked, sealed envelope tucked away in a forgotten ledger. The handwriting was elegant but hurried, revealing plans for a secret meeting by the old mill in North at midnight—a meeting that had been supposedly going on for decades, as the date on the envelope traced back 47 years in the past.

The mention of names but in coded terms hinted at their significance within the town. The list resonated with the one Gio found in Charles's mansion, but the order was different. The initials were new, but one remained the same—*C.B.* In this list, it wasn't at the top but mixed in with the others. This discovery provided the first tangible evidence of the clandestine gatherings that seemed to play a crucial role in the town's hidden dynamics.

Each interview, laced with fear and reluctance, and each step, liberating Gio's mind from the shadow of mystery, added depth to the enigma of Ravenbrook—the mystery surrounding Charles. The silence of its inhabitants spoke volumes, hinting at the darkness that lurked beneath the surface of the murky town. The newly found evidence became a key to the questions that had clouded their minds. Gio and Emily realized that uncovering the truth would require not just skill and determination but also the courage to face the unknown dangers that awaited them.

"How did Charles become the leader with all these above him?" Gio pondered out loud, his eyes wandering through another realm—a realm where new doors to this paradox were opening.

Chapter 7: The Shadows of Ravenbrook

The sky of Ravenbrook darkened with the fog of uncertainties that lay in Gio's quest to seek the truth. Guided by the glimmers of clues illuminated by his unwavering resolve, Gio made progress. He could hear the beat of the heart of this vile creature that had deepened its claws in Ravenbrook's core. He could feel the eeriness of these shadows clinging onto his skin as he pondered over Charles's past life—his journey of rising from the bottom of the list to the top.

"Let us search more. There must be some clues in these dusty ledgers," Emily suggested, coughing from the dust that lingered in the air.

"Search for something that's about decades old. Especially 48-47-year-old newspapers and letters. Someone must have highlighted this if it's as bad as I'm thinking," Gio instructed as he delved into the pile of newspapers.

"You think Charles murdered to get that spot?"

"Either that or he's a really lucky guy," Gio replied faintly.

Silence veiled the room in its tensity; only the crinkling of the pages could be heard as both Gio and Emily buried their consciousness into the search for clues. As he skimmed through the contents of a 30-year-old newspaper, a portrait of his former client printed in it sent a flash of possibility through his mind. Money embezzlement. Gio had cleared that client's name from a money laundering case that seemed unwinnable. A flicker of resolve shot through his eyes as he tethered the threads of silence.

"There's a chance our man didn't only commit murders to rise through ranks."

"What do you mean?" Emily inquired, lifting her eyes from the ledger.

"Money laundering. No matter how many criminals I worked with, murder alone wasn't their motive. There's money involved in every power game," Gio explained.

"He needed to have enough money to make his hold solid over the organization so his authority couldn't be toppled," Emily completed Gio's track of thoughts.

"Exactly!" He remarked, "Let's divide and expedite this. I'll look for the financial discrepancies, and you look for the murder highlights."

"Sounds like a plan," said Emily.

Time trickled through as they continued their search. Minute after minute, the floor began to be blanketed by the newspapers. Slowly, the pile of newspapers and ledgers thinned, but so did the patience of Gio and Emily. Hours had passed, but the clues were yet to be found.

Just when the ray of hope started to diminish from their resolve, Emily huffed.

"We would never find anything like this," she threw her

hands in the air. "I must have searched through millions of papers, but not a single highlight was to be found. They covered their tracks well."

"Same here. I think I feel nauseous reading through tons of murder highlights," Gio sighed.

"Let's see what this last one says. Seems like some sort of scandal of a military official," Emily murmured.

After skimming through its contents, she scrunched the paper and threw it on the ground, startling Gio.

"Simmer down. Was it that bad?" he giggled.

"Just another dirtbag in this town," Emily replied, her complexion dulled in the shades of annoyance.

"Let me see," said Gio as he picked up the paper and skimmed through its contents. "Looks like General Cole wanted to be a billionaire that badly. I-"

"What?" Emily inquired as she looked at Gio's eyes—excitement wrapped in the cloth of anxiousness draped over them.

"G.C.," he mumbled as he stared at the initials written in the article. "These initials…I think I saw them in the old list of names." Hastily, Gio pulled out the list from his pocket—both new and old.

"G.C…G.C…G.C.," he repeated as he ran his finger through the names. "Here!"

There in the top five names on the old list were penned

down the initials that sent shivers down their spine. 'G.C.'. Their consciousness wobbled as they fathomed the depth of the roots that had entangled this town's core.

"If a military official of Cole's rank was a part of this cult, we can't take them as any ordinary one. Looks like Charles was in some deep shit," Gio hypothesized.

"He had embezzled billions of funds according to the allegations thrown by some journalist in that paper. And among them, he was blamed for several murders, but not a single proof was found against him," Emily repeated the contents of the article about him. "Is he on the new list?" She asked—her lips quivered with the fear of knowing the truth.

"At the bottom...," Gio mumbled. Countless theories of murders and conspiracies he had learned of in his career flashed through his mind. "How did someone fall down from the top five to the bottom?"

"Looks like Charles made some enemies in his quest for seeking power," Emily concluded. "Terrifying enemies."

"I believe this was a tactical murder of Charles. They knew what they were doing. They knew the relationship between Nicky and Charles, and it was easy to lay blame on the girl who was painted as a gold digger," Gio rambled out his thoughts.

"Makes sense. They might have created a diversion for the authorities to look away while their mission lay somewhere else," Emily added.

"This is messed up," he whispered, more to himself. "We need to go to the old mill."

"We do? These people seem dangerous, Gio," Emily chuckled weakly.

"They murdered countless people. They looted every person in this town. Your eyes either adjust to the darkness, or you light a candle to get rid of it. It's your choice which one you want to be," Gio retorted as he walked away. "Almost an hour left till midnight. Be on the right side of the history, Emily. Fear is just another emotion. Bury it."

"Always with the word salad," Emily complained under her breath as she followed Gio to his car.

Thanking Diana for her help, Gio and Emily began their journey towards the origins of this mystery. Beneath the night sky and amidst the chirps of crickets, as the distance to their destination neared, the sourness of anticipation cut through their throats. Silence. Fear. Courage.

Their eyebrows knitted together as the blades of the mill came into their vision. A tall ancient mill made of stones stood tall, shadowed by the tall pine trees towering around all its sides. Killing the lights and lowering the speed, they became one with the shadow as embraced in silence, they neared the mill.

"Do you think it has started?" Emily asked, gulping her fears.

"It's already midnight. It should have begun by now.

Let's go," Gio uttered and heaved a sigh, breathing out the anxiety congested in his chest as he stepped out.

"In the open!? What are we some infallible heroes?" Emily yelled in a hushed tone.

"I don't know about you, but I am," Gio chuckled. "Don't worry, we'll sneak into those pine trees up on that hill. The path's covered with trees, so it won't be easy to be found out."

"Alright, let's go," Emily complied as Gio handed her a pitch-black trench coat and wore one himself.

As they became one with the shadow, with light feet, they began to trespass the railing with a 'Private property' signboard on it.

"Remind me to look into who the owner of this mill is," Gio stated as he ventured past the sign.

Nodding along, Emily followed in his footsteps. After crouching through a kilometer of distance, a laser beam swirled through the area. Alerted, both quickly stepped behind the trees as their eyes locked with each other.

"Snipers," Gio murmured.

"I guess this is it," Emily stated in a hefty breath.

"Don't be silly. Let's go. Snipers are on that ramp over the mill. We just need to remember their movement pattern," Gio informed as he began to slither through the trees.

Rubbing her temple in stress, Emily reluctantly followed

Gio as they slithered through the trees. Loud chants reverberated from the ground as they stared—their eyes dry with the danger looming over their senses.

A cluster of men shrouded in dark hoods that veiled their faces stood on the ground while five of them were seated on higher ground, with one man at the top of them all. The mere sight sent shivers down one's spine as the gloominess surrounding that place parched Emily and Gio's throats.

"C-Can you see who's who?" Emily stuttered.

"No. They are covered too well. Their voices are like some hushed chants," Gio replied, his heart frustrated as he didn't want to let this risk and this opportunity go to waste. Hastily, he plucked out his smartphone and opened his camera.

"What are you doing? They might see us!" Emily elbowed him.

"We need to find clues. Sometimes, minor details can reveal the identity of a ghost. As a lawyer, you are mostly chasing ghosts, and those ghosts are always…" Gio stopped as he clicked a photo and continued, "Someone you already know. Remember this ring?"

"That's Milton's ring!" Emily exclaimed.

"Indeed, it is. Let us see who else is here," Gio mumbled as he opened his camera again. As he zoomed in on the person sitting beside who they presumed to be Milton, Gio felt the head of the person tilting in his direction.

'Has he seen me? He looked at me, right?' His thoughts began to scramble as, with shivering hands, he put his phone back.

"Run," he whispered as he took Emily's hand and began to swift through the layers of trees. Dry leaves crunched under their feet as horror flared in his eyes.

"What happened!? Did he see you!?" Emily yelled as her voice shrilled with fear.

"I don't know, and I don't want to wait to find out," Gio retorted as he barged into his car and revved through the streets.

His chest rose up and down as he gasped for breath. His eyes shivered from the emotions that surged through him. His face was drenched with sweat as he reluctantly looked into the rearview mirror. A figure, as if disguised in the cloaks of shadow, stood in the middle of the road—the mere sight of it sent jolts of memory of the figure that lurked around him in Charles's mansion.

As Gio was orienting his disheveled thoughts and emotions, he saw the shadowy figure indulged in his phone. A beep sound erupted from his phone. A text from an unknown sender: *'You have stepped into the world that's not for you, Mr. Gio. There will be consequences, and you will know the terrors of it. Give Nicoletta our best.'*

"No. N-N-No. Not her," Gio mumbled as he switched the gears and bolted through the streets. Hastily, he marched into his house to check up on Nicky. She lay in her bed, eyes closed.

"Nicky! Nicky!!" Tears juggled through his eyes as Gio shoved Nicky. After the third push, she shuffled in her spot. A ripple of relief swept through him as she was just asleep.

"What happened? Are you crying?" Nicky yawned as she blinked at Gio.

"For a moment, I thought I lost you," Gio whispered as he leaned in and embraced her.

In her warmth, his heart found comfort as if every drop of fear evaporated from his entity.

Chapter 8: Threads of Deception

The night sky faded into nothingness as the first rays of the sun broke through, shimmering across the Ravenbrook's murky streets. Gio stood by his bedroom window, his eyes roaming the perimeters of his house. The fear, originating from the last night's threat, trickled through his heart, keeping him awake all night.

Contrary to his suspicions, he couldn't see anyone stalking or patrolling his house. Sighing a breath of relief, Gio averted his eyes towards Nicky, immersing himself in her peacefulness. Pity transformed into relief, relief into affection, and affection into courage as, within moments, his fears vanished as he decided to bring her justice. He remembered his promise and further soldered it with the determination to shield the peacefulness, the serenity that Nicky finally found.

"Morning," Nicky greeted as she descended the stairs.

"Morning to you, too. You're up early," Gio replied as he readied a plate of breakfast.

"Freshly baked croissants? It's been a while since I had these," Nicky mentioned; a smile played on her face as she stared at Gio's back while she ate her breakfast. "Gio, you didn't sleep a wink tonight, and…you were crying last night… What's going on?" She inquired, pouring her curiosity out as Gio's words from last night echoed in her mind.

Silence knitted between them as Nicky's words thwarted Gio's mind back into the events of that night. The cult. The snipers. Milton's ring. The threatening SMS. Flickers of buried emotions draped over Gio's face. His lips voiced silent words but stopped as he concealed his emotions behind the veil of a smile and averted the discussion.

"How are the croissants?" He asked.

"Gio, if something's wrong, you can tell me. It's me," Nicky persuaded, brushing her hand over his.

"I know. It's not that I don't trust you, Nicky. I promised to protect you, and it's just that..." Gio stopped in between his words. His eyes locked with Nicky's while he clasped her hand in his. "...I fear if I tell you and danger finds you because of it, I won't be able to forgive myself," he continued as he kissed her hand.

"Then tell me when you feel the time is right for me to know," Nicky assured him, reflecting a smile at him.

"Carissima, will you honor me with a dance?" Gio said as he bowed and extended his hand toward Nicky.

"I don't see why not, *amorino*," Nicky accepted as she took his hand.

As Italian folk music played over the old gramophone in the living room, Gio and Nicky danced through the empty space, their steps synchronized as their breaths mingled between them. With each step, the burdens over Gio's heart and Nicky's soul dispersed; smiles played on their faces as both drowned in each other's eyes. In the thumping of each other's hearts, they found peace; with each swirl, the dirt of tragedies that befell Nicky vanished as her lively and joyful charisma drenched Gio's heart in even thicker waters of love.

Their steps quickened as the song reached its end; sweat beads, carrying the weight of their worries, trickled down their faces as with their steps in sync, their hands clasped together, they swirled through the room and in a glamorous fashion, Gio swirled Nicky away and pulled her, laying her across his arm. Their hefty breaths scattered across each other's faces as they tied the knot of this exhilarating moment with a kiss.

"Can I ask you something?" Nicky whispered into his ear, her breath still hefty.

"Anything," he responded, grazing her jawline with his finger as he stared into her mesmerizing eyes.

"Please keep yourself safe. Don't get hurt for my sake."

"I promise I will. You take care, too," Gio whispered back.

The evening neared, and Gio's meeting with Emily was nigh. Earlier that day, Emily had texted Gio regarding progress in her discoveries and asked him to meet by the usual café down the street from Charles's mansion. Gio had also spent his day looking into the intricacies of the case, beginning with tracing the unknown phone number that he had entrusted to his former PI. As he laid the groundwork for the finding of the mysterious stalker, Gio scrambled through the articles about General Cole's involvement in the embezzlement of the funds and searched for the pieces of evidence that highlighted his involvement in the Charles's cult.

Tearing through the enigmatic winds of Ravenbrook, Gio's car arrived at the café, and he ventured inside. The bells chimed, announcing his arrival. Amidst the murmurs of the customers, he made his way toward Emily.

"Quite a crowd here," he mentioned as he settled down in his seat.

"Yeah, it's Saturday evening. I'm glad we found a place to sit, at least," Emily responded.

"So, what is it? What did you find out?" Gio asked as he ordered himself a cup of coffee.

"I looked into Milton's past affiliations and any news highlights I could find against him, but the man had a clean record. Nothing. As if everything had been whitewashed…"

"Whitewashed, huh? Well, he definitely has to hide something. But that much we guessed, Emily. What's new?"

"I said nothing because it might have been a regular past for someone, but there was one thing. He has a past with Miss Agnes McAllister," Emily revealed, her voice faint, fading into the chatters of the crowd.

"The woman who testified for Nicky!?" Gio repeated; his interactions with Agnes flickered through his mind.

"Yes. Apparently, Milton and Agnes were a thing of the past. The time when Charles was still in the lower ranks."

"How did you find out?"

"I was looking through Milton's past records I got through my contact in the Police Department, and they said someone filed a complaint of domestic abuse against him years ago, but the details weren't in their records. So, heeding the officer's advice, I marched to the State Archive department and used your name to gain access–"

"My name? That's…"

"Just listen. I'm sorry, but there was no other way. There, I found this case file against Milton filed by Agnes. Apparently, she was trying to put him behind bars or find compensation for his abuse against him."

"What kind of abuse?" Gio inquired, his eyes glimmering with interest as the knots of the mystery were slowly opening.

"Physical. That piece of filth beat her up over some settlement money that was supposed to be divided among them. According to Agnes, a major part of that money was supposed to go to her. I conjectured that if things were playing at this level, then they might have been married in the past or something, but something's definitely fishy there," Emily pondered, anxiety evident on her face.

"How much was the settlement money?" Gio asked, his brows furrowed together while his mind linked together the pieces of this puzzle.

"$100 million."

"W-What!? How did they reach that number for a settlement payment?" Gio's mind throbbed with possibilities and paths that opened before him, each bringing a new light to the mystery before him.

"I don't know. I don't know. Gio, this mess is too much for us alone to deal with. These people are dangerous," Emily poured her worries into her words while she buried her face in her palms. "I stayed up all night thinking of what could possibly be worth this money; what's the connection between Agnes and Milton? But I couldn't. Needless to say, the emotions of that night still haunt my sleep."

"You said it's of the time when Charles was in the lower ranks, right? According to Nicky, Milton, Fredrica, Vince, Alessia, and Wagner were Charles's disciples when he was alive. If this connection goes far back into those times, then this money could have probably been invested in Charles," Gio conjectured as he sipped through his coffee.

"That's a plausible analysis. But how do we go forward from here?"

"We schedule an interview with Miss Agnes and get deeper into this."

"What's to say that she isn't a part of this cult, Gio? We could very well be delivering us to the wolves' den," Emily mentioned.

"Or maybe she had a falling out and could be our way into understanding this cult. It could either deliver us everything or nothing, but we are at risk anyway, Emily. From the moment we set foot near that old mill," Gio highlighted.

"I hate this, but I also want the truth," Emily huffed, but Gio could see her skin paling upon the mention of the old mill.

"Hey, are you alright?" Gio inquired.

"Y-Yeah, I'm fine..." Emily mumbled as she stared out of the window. "In fact, no, I'm not, Gio. Since last night, I felt like I was being followed even in broad daylight. I had to disguise myself and sneak out from the backdoor to come here."

"Hey, it's only a matter of time before we catch them. I know, I felt that fear too, but if we cower against them now, this tragedy will continue to haunt us. Today, it was Nicky; tomorrow, it could be any other innocent soul. Listen, you can stay with us, Emily. I'm sure Nicky won't mind." Gio consoled.

"Don't be ridiculous. I don't want to become a wedge between you two. I can handle myself," Emily scoffed, her words slowly fading away as she lost herself in the fog of worries.

"I haven't told Nicky this yet, but I'm planning to change my house. I'll take Nicky with me, and I'll say you come along also," Gio persuaded, sensing hesitation in Emily's voice.

"Moving? Why and where?"

"They are onto us. If we want to move further, we shouldn't have to worry about ourselves being killed in sleep or something. More than anything, I don't want Nicky to come to harm because of my actions. As for where we would go, come along and find out. We will shift in the middle of the night after ensuring we aren't being stalked."

After contemplating for a while, Emily agreed.

"So, did you find out anything?" She asked Gio.

"Working on something on the side, but mainly, I investigated further into General Cole. His past in the army was pretty convincing. The man had attained medals and everything and excelled in his position, and he was making generous amounts of money. Then I wondered, why does a person like him need to embezzle funds and join the ranks of such people? It doesn't make sense. Was it greed? Was he forced by someone? Did they have something on him? Or did he join the army for a cover? There were too many questions but one answer."

"I researched each aspect in front of me, but nothing could be found. But one thing I learned during all that, hearing his speeches, his interviews, and seeing his letters…it all became clear to me he's a typical narcissist. One thing about narcissists is that they boast, and within that boasting, they reveal something, even if it's minor. Apparently, our general had written an autobiography about himself and his times in wars and all that and how heroic he was, like a messiah for his comrades. He called that book *Heroics of Cole*. Pretty self-absolved, isn't he?"

"Heroics of Cole? Please, that's so cheesy," Emily giggled.

"In that book's chapter on war, he mentioned a comrade who's been with him since the start of his journey in the army. Guess who?" Gio explained.

"Who? Milton?" Emily guessed.

"Close. Wagner. And somehow, what I felt about how he described him was either as if Wagner was his mentor or elder brother. The love, the care, the empathy, the pride with which he described anything about him and how highly he thought of him told me that there was more to it. Their relationship was something I figured brought Cole or Wagner to this cult. Either way, they are connected," Gio spilled the details excitedly, pinpointing each aspect of Cole's involvement.

"Wagner. These disciples of Charles have their hands everywhere," Emily remarked.

"Explains why there was no abysmal reaction to Charles's crowning as the leader. There must be more like this," Gio contemplated.

As their discussion neared its end, the brisk breeze of the night started to swirl through the town, and the fog thickened across the streets. Once they were about to depart, the waitress approached the duo.

"Excuse me, madam, sir. Someone left this for you," she said as she handed over a slip of crinkled paper.

Curiously, Gio and Emily glanced at each other and unfolded the piece of paper. A wave of horror swept through their faces as they read the content of the paper.

'Hello, Mr. Rossi, Ms. Emily. This was quite a meeting, I must say. I wonder what you discussed. I believe I have grown fond of your company, so drive carefully on your way back. It would be a shame to end this companionship so soon...or leave Nicoletta alone in this world, Mr. Rossi.'

Emily's hands shivered as she tucked them away while Gio blankly stared at the letter. His heart quivered with the threat embedded in the words of this letter… Did they plan to execute them on their way home and make it look like an accident? Or was it simply a warning by someone who plans to betray the organization? While his mind roamed through the vague scenarios this threat depicted, Gio understood one thing for certain: The threat was nearing them at a quick pace.

"Did you, um…did you see the person who handed you this?" Gio asked the waitress.

"Yes, sir. A kid handed it to me saying they wanted me to deliver it to you," the waitress explained while she analyzed the conflicted expressions on the duo's faces. "Is everything alright?"

"Y-Yes, yes. I believe it's from someone we know, but we just wanted to be sure. Thanks for the help," Gio said as he tipped the waitress and made his way toward the car. A tinge of frustration boiled inside him as the man who made their nights restless was this close, and he failed to identify him.

"Shouldn't we just walk?" Emily suggested.

"As far as I'm guessing, they are just empty threats for now, Emily. I'm just curious how much they heard," Gio said while his mind wandered through the possibilities of what could happen in the next few moments.

Even though he partially believed what he said, his heart still worried that his enemies had the power to do anything to them, and no one would lift a finger at them.

"I hope you are right, Gio. I truly hope you are…"

Chapter 9: The Rusted Clue

As the birth of the night tinted the skies in its shades, Gio and Emily navigated through the enigmatic streets of Ravenbrook—each turn and each stop at traffic lights spiraled within them the fear, refreshing the threat scribbled in the words of that letter.

Impatience and anxiousness entangled their hearts as their eyes kept ricocheting between the side mirrors and rearview mirror. Each glance focused on detecting the shadowy figure tailing them.

"I told you. Just an empty threat," Gio said as his house neared, and his heart sighed a breath of relief.

Gio's words dissipated into the silence that lingered between them; refusing to respond, Emily kept her senses fixated over the side mirror.

"Turn right from here," Emily uttered, her voice trembling, laced with fear.

"But my house is just two blocks away," Gio replied as confusion trickled through his expression. "Is everything alright?"

"Just turn right. If I'm correct…then we're being followed."

"Are you sure? I didn't notice any," Gio said as he took the turn and peered at the vehicles behind them.

"The rusty classic behind the Rover. I'm sure it took every turn we took behind the cover of traffic," Emily concluded.

"Quite a worn-out car for tailing. Clever," Gio pointed out.

Anxiousness trembled through their hearts as they waited for the suspicious car to take the same turn – impatient to know whether the threat inscribed in that letter was, in fact, real or not. The puttering noise of the car neared—the duo's hearts galloped, beating ferociously as they peered at the intersection. Slowly, the rusty car drove straight onto the street without turning. As soon as relief quelled the anxiousness, Gio's eyes widened; frantically, he switched gears and revved through the streets, drifting through the corners.

"W-What did you see!?" Emily asked worriedly, all the while trying to stabilize herself in her seat.

"He saw. He looked straight at us. He was definitely tailing us," Gio muttered while complex emotions scattered all over his face.

After an hour of scrambling through the maze of Ravenbrook, Gio parked the car in his garage once he was certain he had thrown the stalkers off his tracks. Their breaths hefty, disheveled hair, they marched into the house, and each assumed a position near the window, standing lookout for the lurkers.

"What happened to you two?" Nicky inquired in a hushed

tone as she picked on the scrambled emotions on Gio and Emily's faces.

"Long story, Nicky. I will explain later, but we probably need to go just after midnight," Gio urged.

"Go where?" Nicky asked. "Are they onto us?" She speculated as she sensed the urgency oozing out of Gio's words and his impatient demeanor.

"We are moving to the South. I promise I'll tell you everything, but I want us to be safe first," Gio insisted as he started to pack his belongings. "Emily, stay on the lookout."

Time ticked away as Nicky and Gio, in haste, prepared all their belongings while Emily kept a watch for lurkers. Gio scrambled through the research papers and the bits of evidence he had collected and shoved them into his bag.

"Did you see anyone?" Gio asked as he walked past Emily.

"All quiet. Seems like we are in the clear," Emily responded.

"Alright, there's still half an hour till midnight. We should wait...Nicky, can you switch off the light except for the one in the living room? Let them believe we are at home and preparing to sleep."

Nodding, Nicky complied with Gio's instructions, and the wait began. As they waited, the face of the man in the rusty car flickered through Gio's mind. The wrinkled face with slated eyes shadowed by grey eyebrows.

'Someone that old couldn't possibly be in this tiring

business,' he thought to himself. *'But those eyes...purged from human emotions. I have seen them before...I have felt that before...the coldness and bloodlust...The day I met Emily in Charles's mansion...yes...it's those eyes that stared at me from across the street.'*

Roaming through his thoughts, Gio gathered the pieces of the past encounters with the lurker. *'The first one was around Charles's mansion. The second one was near the mill. The third time the stalker appeared was when Emily uncovered Cole and Agnes's possible relationship. And then in the café near Charles's residence and tailing us afterward.'*

'There has to be something in all this...something common,' Gio stressed as he gazed at each piece through his mind's eye.

Beginning from the first encounter at Charles's mansion, he scoured through the memories of that day. The blood stains were cleaned from everywhere else, but the drapes and the dried blood on the sign carved on the floorboard. *'At that time, my hunch was that someone left it as a souvenir. Let's start with that.'*

"If someone leaves something like that, they leave signs where they could see them like an artist's admiration toward his art. But they wouldn't risk going back to the scene of the crime. It's just too much effort and risk… Maybe someone who lives nearby?" Gio mumbled to himself.

Something clicked in his mind as slowly, the pieces of the puzzle began to form a certain shape—the shape of the person who might be a part of it. The clock hand struck the hour of 12:30, sounding the alarms in everyone's heads—it was time to leave.

"Gio, it's time," Emily reminded.

Pausing his track of thoughts, Gio skimmed his gaze through the streets once more – it was empty. Loading their belongings in the vehicle, the trio made their way to their new home.

"Nicky, I asked Emily to live with us till this matter's over. She's been stalked, and I figured it would be wise to keep our allies close... I hope you don't mind," Gio whispered to Nicky.

"Of course, I don't. It's only rational," Nicky smiled.

Reflecting a smile back, Gio steered through the abandoned streets under the veil of night. After an hour of journey, the landscape changed—tall trees shadowed the bumpy dirt road, and a refreshing breeze, purged of the murkiness of the Ravenbrook, swirled.

"Don't tell me this God-awful road is the only one leading to the estate," Emily complained as she jolted left and right.

"It's not...if you can climb those trees, that is," Gio snickered.

"Funny. I feel like I'm gonna vomit my innards out at this rate," Emily huffed.

"She's right, Gio. This terrain is awful," Nicky added as her face turned red, barely holding back the urge to puke.

"Well, consider it a trial to relish the comfort of the estate. It'll blow your minds," Gio boasted as he giggled under his breath after seeing Emily and Nicky's expressions.

After a cloud of dust dissipated and the blanket of trees thinned, the view of the estate came into view – an old building made of stones and its design told as if it had been standing there since the Roman times with a little pond beside it. A smirk crossed Gio's face as he peered at his companions, gauging their emotions—a look of disappointment flickered in their eyes while they faked smiles so as not to tarnish Gio's excitement.

"T-Totally worth it," Emily stuttered.

"Yeah, it seems peaceful…" Nicky added.

"Alright, you don't have to fake it. It's safe here, at least," Gio concluded as they all began to unload.

After everyone settled in the new place, they held a meeting by the fireplace, sipping through their coffees. The puzzle that Gio was solving before flashed through his mind while Emily stared at him as if waiting for him to start explaining the matter to Nicky. Taking the hint, Gio began.

"Since I promised to explain everything to you once we settled here, here it is, Nicky. Before I start, just know that I would never let any harm come to you."

"I know, Gio," Nicky replied, her eyes embracing the essence of a smile as she looked at Gio while her heart throbbed impatiently for the details.

Beginning from the night Gio met Emily, he poured every incident that had taken place and the intricacies of their investigation before Nicky. Explaining their encounter with the stalker at the mill and the possibility of Milton and other disciples of Charles being the main organizers of this organization. With each detail, Nicky's expressions changed from fear to pain, from pain to empathy, as she heard how close to danger Gio was. As Gio finished, Nicky stood from her spot and embraced him. In that moment, each fear and worry that had made a home in Gio's heart evaporated into the mist of love.

"Uhm, alright, so what's our next step? We can't stay down here forever," Emily interjected.

"Before that, thank you for everything, Emily," said Nicky, slightly bowing her head.

"It's the least I could do for justice to prevail…anyways, what about interviewing Miss Agnes, Gio? I thought we would go to her before coming here."

"About that… Before leaving, I thought for a while. You might have been right, Emily. We should take our time before interviewing her," Gio vaguely answered.

"Why? Did you find something?"

"I'll tell you when I'm sure. Some things still don't make sense about her," Gio replied as his eyebrows knitted together, the thought of that bloodstained drape etched in his mind.

"Maybe we should make a team. The three of us can't

cover everything, and by the looks of it, we don't have much time," Nicky chimed in.

"Are you sure you want to be a part of it, Nicky? You'll be jeopardizing your safety."

"Actually, since we had that talk with Milton and others, I investigated them on my own. I sensed something fishy about their behavior… They were too confident now, but before Charles, they seemed tame. So, I couldn't sit back and watch it being played," Nicky revealed while Gio and Emily looked at her in awe.

"This is…surprising. How did you manage alone? It's too dangerous, Nicky," Gio rambled; his words embodied his confusion.

"I wasn't working alone. Hence, part of the reason I suggested the idea of working as a team."

"I'm now seeing you in a new light," Emily muttered as specks of admiration flickered in her eyes. "I say it's a brilliant idea. So, what did you find?"

"So far, my contacts unraveled one of Charles's hideouts in Southeast, the outskirts of Ravenbrook. Probably around here somewhere. Due to some movement there, they couldn't infiltrate the hideout, but there was something of importance there since there were guards patrolling the area. I have been meaning to get into that place for some time now, but I couldn't find any opportunity," Nicky poured the information before them.

"A hideout of Charles? That's a big find, Nicky. You are right. If he didn't tell you about this, then it must have something to do with his cult," Gio thought out loud. "Can you bring your team here? We can use valuable people who share the same cause as us."

"I have known them since before I was with Charles, so they value my cause. I can surely call them… After all, it's been long since I met them in person," Nicky said as her mind wandered through the memories of the past. A sense of longing adorned her eyes.

"If you trust them, then we can trust them. Let's call them," Gio decided as the others agreed.

As the trio's resolve to unravel the threads of this mystery gained a new spark, dawn broke through the skies, shedding away the darkness of the night. Gio found a flicker of hope in the new perspective he gained in light of the pieces of the puzzle left behind by the murderer of Charles and the stalker.

The newborn sun, the slowly dispersing fog around the trio's new home, the new clue found by Nicky, and the addition of teammates marked the beginning of a new journey—a journey that Gio was determined to cover with courage and find justice that had been buried under the rotten bones of Ravenbrook for a long time.

Chapter 10: The Masked Agenda

As the sun shimmered across the land and the chirping birds induced a tinge of serenity in the air, Gio sat across the old television, switching through channels, frustrated at the static screen. The signal reception at the outskirts of Ravenbrook was a disaster, as it was during his father's time.

"Come on, come on!" Gio mumbled to himself as he adjusted the antennas.

"Didn't know you had a thing for antiques," Emily chimed in as she slumped into the sofa.

"I don't. It's been ages since last I came here," Gio responded.

"I mean, I know we joked about it, but it's quite peaceful here. No blaring honks, but sweet melodies of the birds. Instead of tall buildings, it's trees," Emily said, taking in a deep breath, relishing the peacefulness.

"What's your point?"

"My point is, why didn't you come here? If I had something like this, I would never abandon it."

Gio remained silent as his eyes embossed with emotions of regret and pain. Realizing the effect of her words, Emily coughed.

"I-I didn't mean to be nosey. Sorry."

"It's fine," Gio sighed.

Moments after, the static buzz vanished, and the voice of a news anchor erupted from the TV. "Finally, I-" Words betrayed his thoughts as his eyes fixated on the headline.

"Two bodies were found by the townspeople near the creek flowing in the North of Ravenbrook. Upon police's arrival, the bodies were identified to be Mr. Jeremy Denver, the foreign minister, and his personal bodyguard. The police investigations suggest that the bodies were thrown into the creek from somewhere along the North mill."

"J.D.," Gio mumbled, his senses scattered all over the place as shock consumed him.

"What?"

"The list, Emily. Do you have it?"

"Y-Yeah, let me go grab it," Emily stuttered as she trod towards her room. Stopping in her tracks, her shaky voice rose again. "Um, which one?"

"Both."

Shortly after, Emily walked in with the lists in her hand, Nicky alongside her. With a pale face, hands shaking, and lips quivering, Emily stood in her place. "I-I-It can't be, right?"

"What? What happened?" Nicky inquired, confused by the stern expression on Gio's face and Emily's despair.

Without replying, Gio pointed towards the TV while he skimmed through the lists. 'J.D.' the initials of the foreign minister were penned on both lists – the old and the new one.

While his heart trembled upon confirmation, his mind throbbed over the intensity of the crisis, the danger that loomed over Ravenbrook—over them. The thought of politicians being in the same league as Charles and with the military personnel part of it, too, captivated Gio's resolve, clarifying before him the risk he and his team carried.

"They just murdered a prominent political figure…and that, too, of their own league," Emily rambled.

"Charles was one of them, too. They killed him, but this… It must have some repercussions if the government decides to investigate," Nicky voiced her opinion.

"That's true unless the government is in their pockets," Gio contemplated.

Suddenly, his phone chimed—a text from Milton—the disciple who seemed to be the leader of Charles's organization: *"Let us meet, Mr. Rossi. It's been long. And please, don't bring Nicky this time. I'll be waiting at Pamela's café by York Street at 3 pm. Don't be late."*

It was as if the pieces that Gio had fitted together began to fall apart once again and scatter. The sight of the hooded figure, sitting on the top seat, whom Gio caught on his camera at the North Mill, flickered before his eyes. His consciousness was confiscated in the fetters of confusion as nothing made sense anymore.

'*Why is he inviting me? Does he plan to be rid of me? No, he chose a public place. Maybe he wants to be sure whether I know of his identity or not,*' Gio lost himself in the fog of thoughts as his mind couldn't navigate towards a certain conclusion. '*Should I go or not?*'

"Who is it? You seem as if a ghost texted you," Nicky inquired while Emily sat silently, staring coldly at the TV.

"A ghost, huh? You are probably right," Gio replied while his thoughts whispered to him, '*Maybe it's time to bring the ghost to light. Such opportunity may not arrive again in the future, and I need to lure the information out of him.*'

At that moment, Gio fortified his resolve as he made his decision to meet with Milton.

"Who is it, Gio?" Nicky asked again.

"A friend for now, I suppose," Gio lied as he couldn't let Nicky know of this, or she would stop him. "Alright, Emily and you," Gio continued, but Emily remained unresponsive. "Hey, Emily! Snap out of it. We'll catch them. All of them, but I need you to be your best self. You and Nicky should go and see what you can find regarding Jeremy's murder. Any little detail might be the piece missing in this puzzle."

"And you?" Emily responded.

"I have a meeting. An important one."

Wearing a French-blue suit, paired with a stainless white shirt and oxford boots, Gio readied for the meeting—practicing the questions and counter-questions, going through the plan to trap Milton in the snare of words.

"Make sure to go out the back door and take the narrow road out. We can't leave tracks for them to find us here," Gio instructed as he marched down the stairs.

"There was another road!? And you brought us from that forsaken one?" Emily ranted.

"Well, you will wish to be on that 'forsaken' road once you see the other one," Gio smirked.

"Be safe!" Nicky yelled from behind.

"You too," Gio smiled, waving goodbye.

Changing the tires exclusive to his model of car and replacing the license plate, Gio drove out towards Pamela's Café. It was 2:43 pm; the sun blazed over Ravenbrook while the trees gently swayed as he waited in his car. His heart thumped with anxiousness—a pressure that parched his throat, a feeling that he only felt during Nicky's trial.

Fear.

Fear of losing everything.

For 17 minutes, he sat in his car seat, wandering his gaze around the nearby sidewalks and buildings to see if Milton had arranged any hitmen, but he couldn't find a trace of any suspicious soul.

As the clock hit 2:59, Nicky's voice resounded in Gio's head, dispersing the plague of worries that suffocated his resolve. Embedding confidence in his stride, Gio walked into the café – a dimly lit room with sunlight veiling it in a light orange shade as it refracted through the tinted windows. A noble-looking crowd, dressed in formal attire filled the café while Gio's eyes ricocheted from one table to another, searching for Milton.

"Señor Giuseppe Rossi?" The waiter asked.

"That's me, yes," Gio answered.

"This way, sir. Señor Milton is waiting for you in the VIP room."

Sighing, Gio strode towards the VIP room, following the waiter's lead. As he ventured through the hallway, his eyes skimmed through several notable figures – higher-ups of political parties and military, along with businessmen and police, conversed joyously with each other in the segregated lobbies.

'What are they all doing here laughing when the fricking Foreign minister was just murdered?' Gio's heart, infuriated, whispered to his mind.

Navigating through the candlelit hallway—each flame akin to Gio's emotions, he arrived at the VIP room. Heaving out a sigh, blowing away the burning emotions into thin air, sharpening his mind with rationality and courage, Gio marched inside and started the recording on his phone. Holding a glass of whiskey in his hand, wearing a gold ring with the letter 'M' carved with diamonds on it, and dressed in a gentleman's suit from Victorian times sat Milton.

"Finally, we meet at last. You are five minutes late, Mr. Rossi," Milton's coarse voice echoed in the room.

"Apologies for the delay, though. I must say you look quite sharp, Mr. Milton," Gio said, taking a seat across the table.

"To be a gentleman, you have to dress like one, Mr. Rossi. You must know this yourself for a person who has a collection of such fine-tailored suits," Milton complimented, sipping through his whiskey while his eyes analyzed Gio up and down.

"You are quite right about that. Those tattered jeans cannot elevate a man's elegance but degrade it, I must say," Gio responded, his eyes fixated on Milton's ring.

'The same ring...' he thought to himself.

"It was gifted to me by Master Charles. A bit shiny piece, but I have come to cherish it," noticing Gio's gaze, Milton said as he caressed the ring.

"Looks good. So, I'm quite curious why you asked me here today, Mr. Milton?" Gio finally asked the question that was entrenched in his mind, birthing more questions but no answer.

"Well, I quite liked you the last time we met. So, I thought, why not meet again," Milton smirked, gazing into Gio's now even more confused eyes.

"I would have taken it as a compliment if it were true, Mr. Milton. You have a way with jokes; I'll give you that," Gio sighed.

"Haha! You are a sharp kid. We'll come to the reason later. First, tell me, how's Nicoletta faring?"

"She's recovering. I'm surprised by how fast she recovered. Usually, people tend to seek revenge from the people who framed them," Gio replied; Milton's face twitched for a second. Though his heart ached by seeing Milton's audacity, his mind prepared to ensnare him into the trap where he might reveal something admissible in the court.

"Nicoletta's a strong girl, Mr. Rossi. Don't mix her up with the rest of the bunch. She, after all, spent time with Charles," Milton added as he lit his cigar. "Cuban?"

"I'll take one," Gio agreed as he took the cigar. "I presumed she was not involved in Charles's matters."

"Part of the reason I asked you to come alone, Mr. Rossi. You are right. Charles didn't let her be a part of our business, but she had her own crew working from overseas and dealing with a portion of Charles's business," Milton explained while Gio, though conflicted about the authenticity of Milton's information, kept a straight face.

"I heard they are quite a talented bunch. Nicky told me about them," Gio replied confidently, dismissing Milton's attempts to draw a line between Gio and Nicky.

"Quite an enviable bond you two share. So, tell me, Mr. Rossi, what are you up to these days? I drove past your apartment the other day, but it seemed like you guys weren't home."

'I see why he called me here. He was anxious. He couldn't keep track of us anymore, so he wanted to meet me. Clever old man,' Gio scoffed under his breath.

"Nothing much, Mr. Milton. A lawyer rarely gets the time

to afford the peace of home. Have you heard about the foreign minister, though?" Gio inquired, his eyes preying upon Milton's expressions, searching for hints.

"Indeed, I did. Poor soul did not deserve such an ending," Milton sighed as he got up from his seat and ventured towards the window, blowing out wisps of smoke. "I reckon he put his hands where they didn't belong. Such is the world of Ravenbrook."

"What do you mean?"

"Do you know Albert Camus, Mr. Rossi?"

"Never heard of him," Gio replied, rowing along the flow of conversation.

"He once said the slave begins by demanding justice and ends by wanting to wear the crown. He must dominate in his turn," Milton quoted, spouting each word with passion while Gio picked up on the warning veiled under the eloquent words.

"You think Mr. Jeremy conspired for a higher seat?"

"Who knows? I'm just an old man spewing what I learned with the wisdom of age, Mr. Rossi."

"They say his body was probably thrown in the creek from somewhere near the Northern mill. It's such an eerie spot. Have you been there, Mr. Milton?" Gio asked, luring Milton.

A hint of unease scattered over Milton's face; his hands clenched behind his back so tight that his nails etched in his palms while he blew out a cloud of smoke. Heaving out a sigh, Milton turned to Gio.

"I have indeed heard the ominous rumors surrounding that place. But in the end, they are just rumors, Mr. Rossi. Rumors spread by hooligans who don't know their place," Milton spoke, his voice low but growling with anger and frustration. Picking up on the little clues Milton left, Gio penned them in his mind's diary.

"You know, there's a line pretty famous in my line of field. If a rumor is repeated by everyone, it eventually becomes the truth," Gio said, adding fuel to the flame of anger he sensed in Milton, for anger kills the rationality of many a person.

"Are you insinuating something, Mr. Rossi?" Milton asked in a low voice, putting out his cigar.

"Why would you think that, Mr. Milton?"

"Haha! I see you never leave the courtroom, Mr. Rossi. Since you have turned this room into one, too, I must disclose something. The reason I called you here," Milton steered away from the conversation as he sensed something amiss in Gio's words.

"I'm all ears, Mr. Milton."

"I know who killed Jeremy Denver."

Chapter 11: Web of Lies

'Why is he revealing the murderer? Isn't it him? Does he plan to lure me away from his tail?'

A cluster of thoughts fogged Gio's mind upon hearing Milton's words. His mouth was left open, his eyes lost in the realm of possibilities, searching for the meaning behind Milton's intentions.

"You seem shocked, Mr. Rossi. It's been years since I saw you this bewildered. Almost as if you lost him again," said Milton, smirking.

"H-How do you know?" Gio asked, confused about how Milton knew of the incident related to his father, his mind drowning in the flood of abstractions.

"Come now, Mr. Rossi. Surely, a man of my standing knows this much… I have my sources," Milton huffed.

"Excuse me for the misjudgment, but I thought you stayed clear of such matters," holding the reins of his rationality, reminding himself of his purpose, Gio discussed.

The curiosity of knowing who Milton would name as the murderer of Jeremy Denver increased with every passing moment, but Gio focused on his primary goal: extracting as much information from Milton as he could.

"Once you stand amongst the leaders, Mr. Rossi, you naturally learn the art of obtaining sensitive information. Or else, you are the one licking their boots," Milton answered vaguely.

"How did you know Jeremy Denver?"

"You are not asking the right questions, Mr. Rossi. The question you need to ask is: *Who killed him?*" Milton retorted, flicking off the ash of his cigar into the ashtray.

"I'm the sort who saves the good part of the food till last, Mr. Milton. However, I'll change my question, respecting the fact that you are the host. Do you know what all those government officials are doing here at such a critical time?" Inquired Gio as he leaned back into his chair.

"Drinking, whoring, conspiring…What else did you expect from such corrupt trash, Mr. Rossi? I'll tell you this: no one in that room would do anything for justice. They move where the wind blows," Milton opinioned.

Gio sat in silence, staring into Milton's sleek eyes while he contemplated his words. He wasn't lying, but he hated them.

'Maybe Jeremy was a part of that room, too, once. A thorn in Milton's side,' Gio thought to himself.

Words chosen by Milton showed his hatred, but more so, his authority over them as if they were nothing in his eyes. *'I suppose by 'Wind' he meant power—himself.'* As Gio readied to put forward his next question, a knock on the door interrupted his flow.

"Sir, they are waiting for you," the waitress informed.

'They? Who? The other disciples? Or the officials in the other room? I needed more time!' A hint of panic jolted Gio's mind as he saw Milton readying to leave.

"Alright, hon'. I'll be there," Milton replied as he strolled away. "Oh, Mr. Rossi, since you forgot to ask again, consider this a thank you for accepting my invitation. It's Cole...General Cole. Have a pleasant night," Milton revealed as he walked away with a smile.

"W-Wait, wait! General Cole!?" Gio yelled, but Milton vanished into the hallway.

A storm of conflictive emotions swirled through Gio as not one part of him was prepared for what Milton revealed. He just ratted out his own accomplice—one of his own people.

Hastily, Gio rushed out, eager to confirm the authenticity of Milton's information. The clouds of a thunderstorm veiled the starry sky of the night as the rain pattered across the city; he drifted towards his estate in the South.

"What is he planning? What the fuck is he planning? First, Jeremy Denver and now, he plans to get rid of General Cole? Why? Why!?" Gio screamed inside his car as he raced through the streets.

Lost in the haze of reasons for Milton's recent actions, Gio's mind blanked, warping into the wormhole of the past—a moment where he sat by his father's deathbed, but instead of the young boy he once was, he found his current self conversing with his father.

"You look lost, mio figlio," his father said, his voice frail but filled with empathy.

"Dad...I...I...," Gio stuttered; something inside him broke...again as tears welled up in his eyes.

"It wasn't your fault, Gio. I'm proud of you for standing up for justice. Sometimes, it comes with a price, but that's the beauty of it, son. You stand up for it despite the scars it carved onto your soul. You are a brave child... You always have been," his father said, caressing Gio's face.

Sniffling through his tears, gulping the sadness overwhelming him, Gio uttered, "Dad, there's this woman I love. I love her so dearly that each moment I spend with her heals every scar I have. Someone framed her for murder, but the ones who did...sit too far from my reach. Mocking me as I dance their dance."

"Son, there are people who emerge in your life as a poem – a poem the universe wrote to keep you alive, and each verse would breathe purpose in your defeated heart. For me, it was your mother. For you, it's this woman. Believe in the love, and you will see walls as high as the sky crumbles before you."

Slowly, Gio's vision blurred as the sight of his father began to dissolve into a mist with an echo of his last words resounding in Gio's mind, "I believe you will find justice...even if it's eons away from you... You, my son, will find it."

As he hit a bump on the road, his consciousness drifted

back to reality. Sweat dripped from his chin as tears dried on his cheeks, but in his mind, he felt the clarity with which he started this pursuit of justice. Burying the emotions of the past, deriving clues from Milton's veiled derogatory remarks, Gio, with a newly found resolve, drove through the muddy pathway leading to his estate.

"Gio! What took you so long?" Nicky inquired as soon as Gio entered the house.

"The interview…it kind of stretched long, but I have some solid inform—" Gio stopped midways as he wandered his gaze around, noticing some new faces.

"Hey, Mr. Rossi. We meet at last. Nicky told us a lot about you. I'm Claire," Claire, one of the new team members who worked with Nicky, introduced herself.

"Um, hi, Claire. Good to meet you," Gio shook her hand.

"Sorry, I forgot to introduce you guys. That's Brian over there. That's Julian. You already met Claire, and that's Keisuke," Nicky introduced them, pointing towards each new member.

"It's a pleasure to meet you all. Hope you find this place comfortable," Gio greeted them.

"Not a countryman I am, but this place is sugoi!" Keisuke, a 24-year-old boy with dyed teal hair, yelled ecstatically.

"Um, *sugoi*? What's that?"

"It's Japanese for 'amazing.' Ignore him. He's a bit too

energetic but valuable," Nicky whispered to Gio.

Meanwhile, Brian and Julian glued their eyes to the TV, unbothered by the presence of Gio. Heaving out a sigh, Gio asked.

"Where's Emily?"

"She's in her room. Researching something she said she found related to Agnes," Nicky replied.

"Alright, we need to round everyone up. I think I have a plan," Gio instructed.

Moments later, everyone gathered in the living room and Gio, piecing together a plan from the newly discovered pieces of the puzzle, began his address. He brought the new members of the squad up to pace as he told them about their past investigations, interactions and the dangers this pursuit possessed.

"Alright, today I met with Milton and—"

"Wait, Milton, the one we are chasing? Did you mean him when you mentioned *a friend for now,* huh?" Emily interjected.

"Wait, let me finish first. I know how reckless it sounds, but he chose a public place, and it was a perfect opportunity to learn more about them."

"So, what did you learn, tomodachi?" Keisuke asked.

"Is he always this cringy?" Emily whispered to Claire. Defeatedly, she shrugged in response.

"The identity of the murderer of Jeremy Denver. It's General Cole, according to Milton."

"Wait…it doesn't make sense. Cole!? Why would Milton give him away just like that?" Emily asked.

"Maybe he has found some new motive. Or he plans to get rid of those who pose a threat to his leadership," Nicky evaluated.

"Makes sense. He doesn't want what happened to Charles to happen to himself," Claire added.

"What do we know of this Cole guy?" Brian asked.

"Good question, Brian. We know he's been involved in the embezzlement of the funds, and he's an opportunist plus an egomaniac. Too self-absorbed, but something kept him timid when it came to Charles's disciples like in his autobiography," Gio explained.

"And he's cautious and makes calculated moves. If he really did murder Jeremy, there must be a reason why he dumped his body from near the mill," Julian opinioned.

"So, what's the plan?" Nicky asked.

"The plan is that we leave Milton alone, for now. We should start by cutting off people from his organization one by one, even if it's someone who's on bad terms with him. When he's left at the top alone, he would be easy to subdue, but right now, he's untouchable," Gio poured the plan before his team, awaiting their response.

"We force him out of the shadows in which he hides and

put him in the sunlight. That seems like a reasonable plan to me," Nicky acknowledged.

"I'm in, too."

"Me too."

"Count me in."

"What about you, Julian?" Gio asked as he remained the only one silent.

"I'm thinking…what if we threaten Cole with how we know of his secret and how Milton has abandoned him? He'll surely know something valuable that might help us get Milton and the other disciples much more easily," Julian contemplated.

"I thought about that, but it carries too much risk. If the information Milton gave us turns out to be false, we would be delivering ourselves to Cole on a silver platter. Letting an enemy into our circle would be catastrophic, so we gather evidence and let justice do its work," Gio replied as his father's last words echoed in his mind—a ripple of pain swept through his face.

"I agree with him. We cannot trust Milton's words blindly. We need to gather some evidence to prove Cole is the murderer, and then we will play our cards accordingly," said Emily.

"Alright, tomorrow, we each divide into three teams and search everything we can find about Cole," Gio said, adjourning the meeting as he retired to his room.

The events that transpired during the day circulated through his mind. Tiredness crawled through his marrow, but the will that flickered under the winds of stress to find Nicky justice and liberate her of the fetters of accusations and shame poured upon her by society flickered brighter than ever in his heart. With a knock on the door, Nicky entered the room.

"Hey, are you alright? You seemed…distressed for a moment out there," she inquired.

"So, you noticed," Gio chuckled. "Come, lay down," he said, and Nicky hopped onto the bed. Cuddling her, Gio continued, "I just remembered my father's words. There were some things Milton said that made me remember him."

"You never told me about your father? What happened to him?" Nicky asked.

Heaving out a sigh, Gio said, "It's just…it's a part of my life I never disclose to others. But to you, I will when the time is right."

"I don't mean to pry. I just want you to know that I'll be with you no matter what. No matter what stands in our way, I'll find my way to you because you found me when the world had abandoned me," Nicky's voice, her words like a lullaby, instilled peace in his soul—peace sprouted from the roots of love.

"I promise to tell you everything once this is all over, and I can ask you to be the part of my soul that was always missing," Gio whispered.

Giggling, Nicky leaned closer to Gio's face, their breaths intertwined and whispered back:

"I'll wait for that day, and till that day and the days to come, you'll always have my love."

Chapter 12: Truth or Consequences

Leaves rustled, and dust arose from the impatient feet. Sunlight shimmered through the swaying trees as a squad navigated through the dense forest surrounding an isolated cabin.

"Guards on 11 o'clock," Brian whispered into his walkie-talkie.

"What's the plan?" Julian asked as he, Brian, and Claire took their spots in the forest, hiding in the shadows while their eyes scanned the area brimming with guards equipped with sub-machine guns.

"The plan? I say we create a distraction, and Julian knocks them out from behind," Brian suggested.

"A solid plan," Claire added.

"Hey, hey, weren't you guys in the military once? What sort of plan is this? Putting me alone in that den of death?" Julian complained.

"Well, will you be the decoy then?" Claire retorted.

Amidst the gentle breeze, silence lingered through the radio line for some time.

"I-I guess the first plan sounds pretty good," Julian stuttered. His eyes heavied under the sweat dripping from his forehead while Brian and Claire prepared their distraction plan.

"Two guards at the front. Three in the back. Alright...Let's do this," Brian uttered.

"Let's just hope there's not any inside the cabin," Julian muttered.

"Pessimist," Claire scoffed as she readied her arsenal. "Let's do it."

Stealthily, Brian slithered through the forest, taking his position towards North. Once at his position, he alerted the guards by snapping some twigs, rustling the leaves in the ground, and letting out screams of pain—orchestrating a scenario as if someone had fallen from the trees. Alarmed by the presence of someone in the cabin's vicinity, the guards moved in the direction of the screams.

"You two, stay here," one of the guards commanded as the three guarding the rear of the house marched away.

"God help me," Julian prayed as he readied his sleeping darts.

In a swift motion, he blew the darts, and each dart was injected into the guard's neck. Drowsiness clouded their minds as both fell lifelessly onto the ground while the other three neared Brian, scouring through the bushes and searching for Brian. Covertly, Claire from the East and Brian from the West snuck behind the guards, twisting their necks while Julian put the third one to sleep with one of his darts.

"That went...smooth," Julian commented, a grin of relief plastered over his face.

"It always goes smoothly. You just like to rant like a baby," Claire retorted, giving Julain a side-eye.

"They won't be asleep for eternity, you know. Stop your bickering, and let's tie 'em up," Brian ordered as he stepped away, radioing Gio and the others waiting in their car a mile away from the cabin.

"It's clear."

Twigs crunched underfoot as Gio and the team approached the cabin, their breaths steady with anticipation. Gio's heart pounded against his ribcage as he led the way, his senses heightened by the gravity of their mission – the anticipation of what secrets Charles's cabin held for him.

As they neared the cabin, Gio's eyes caught sight of Brian and the others just ahead, partially obscured by the thick foliage. "There," he whispered to Nicky, gesturing towards the cabin with a nod.

Nicky nodded in acknowledgment, her gaze fixed on the cabin while her heart thrummed the same beat as Gio's heart—the beat of anxiousness and determination.

"They are quite the bunch you have gathered there, Nicky," Gio whispered into Nicky's ear.

"Well, they once worked for Charles, so…" Nicky shrugged with a smirk.

"Neat. Let's go see what's inside."

As Gio entered the worn-out cabin, the air was heavy with anticipation. He and the others scattered their eyes around the timber interior, which was infected with mold. A musty smell suffocated Emily.

"This is horrible. As if someone left bodies to rot here," Emily complained.

"Tell me about it," Claire added as Emily retched on the side.

"Alright, I'll be waiting outside. I can't stand it, or I'll vomit my guts out," Emily said as she ventured outside.

The squad scoured through each nook and cranny of the cabin but was unable to find anything relevant to what they hoped to acquire. Minutes kept sifting through; a storm brewed outside, and the sky darkened as they kept on looking. As the first drops of rain pattered on the ground, Julian yelled as he lay on the floor.

"There's something here." He strived to pluck the floorboard off. It didn't take long for them to uncover a hidden compartment beneath the floorboards containing a trove of documents and files.

Gio's hands trembled slightly as he pulled out the first document, his eyes scanning the pages with a mix of determination and dread. Nicky stood beside him, her expression a mirror of his own, as they delved into the secrets hidden within the papers.

"This...this is huge," Nicky murmured, her voice barely above a whisper as she took in the implications of what they were uncovering. "Everything here points towards

Vince…I-Is Milton just a pawn here? And all these properties… They belonged to Charles…"

Gio nodded grimly, his mind racing as he pieced together the puzzle before them. "It seems that way," he agreed, his voice heavy with the weight of their discovery.

Every estate, business, and charity organization that fell under Charles now had Vince's name as the sole owner inked instead. *'Everything Milton said, every single word…was it just a ruse planned by Vince all along? But why was Milton sitting in the top seat at the meeting?'* Disheveled questions haunted Gio's mind one after another.

"Look for General Cole's records. If he murdered Jeremy, then he most likely is the hitman of the organization, and he would have murdered someone before, too," Gio said as he skimmed through a pile of files before him.

"Um, Nicky… I think there's dirt on everyone here," Claire murmured from the side.

"What do you mean?" Brian asked.

"I mean, they have evidence of everyone in their organization…except for the disciples."

A ripple of excitement gushed through Gio's heart as he read through the titles of each page, highlighting the names of each member of the group.

"This…this is marvelous! There's enough evidence here to put them all behind bars," Gio chuckled.

"But not the disciples," Nicky chimed in, her voice low.

"Consider this organization as a behemoth. If we get rid of these people, this behemoth would be crippled. Cutting off its limbs, we would immobilize it, and they would be easy and vulnerable to go after," Gio explained.

Among the documents, they found damning evidence linking General Cole to the organization, detailing his role in various illegal activities.

"This implicates Cole directly," Gio said, his voice filled with a mix of anger and determination as he held up a ledger that documented payments from Cole to known associates of the organization. "It's solid proof of his involvement. Look here: his victims are found missing vital organs. Do you remember what Jeremy's body looked like? Multiple stab wounds near the heart area and ruptured lungs plus near his eye sockets."

"He was trying to carve them out but was interrupted," Julian concluded.

"Exactly," Gio agreed.

"When you think this man can't get any more disgusting, he does," Nicky grunted.

"He's operating some organ donor hospital, too," Brian revealed as he read through another document.

"There's more. He has shares, multiple shares, in Vince's companies and has laundered billions through them."

"If not for murder, we can take him down for laundering, but this man needs to be behind bars as soon as possible,"

Gio remarked, specks of anger scattered over his face while his eyes shone with determination.

But perhaps most intriguing of all was a small hint regarding the McAllister family, buried within the pages of a seemingly innocuous report related to General Cole.

"Look at this," Claire said, her voice tinged with excitement as she pointed to a line of text that mentioned a connection between the McAllisters and a shell company linked to Cole's donor organization. "It's a small clue, but it could be the key to unraveling the mystery surrounding the McAllister family."

"McAllister? Agnes McAllister... Everything is fishy around that woman, Gio," said Nicky.

"Does it say the first name?" Gio asked.

"Just McAllister.'

"Why? Why would she help Nicky when she was a part of it?" Gio thought out loud.

"Maybe Nicky's apprehension was a distraction they needed. Once the deed was done, Agnes stepped in and became the heroine of justice—a clever move to rid herself of any suspicions," Claire suggested.

"It's not entirely impossible. She is a clever woman, after all," Gio agreed while the suspect he had in mind for the puzzle that plagued his mind for days—the puzzle of bloodstained drapes and carvings... His resolve to conduct a meeting with her solidified.

As they gathered up the documents, preparing to leave the cabin behind, Gio couldn't shake the feeling that they were on the brink of uncovering something much bigger than they had ever imagined. With each piece of the puzzle they uncovered, the truth seemed to inch closer, beckoning them into the heart of the mystery that had consumed their lives.

As they meticulously combed through the documents strewn across Charles's cabin, each page revealed a layer of the intricate web of deceit woven throughout Ravenbrook. Gio and his team exchanged knowing glances as they pieced together the puzzle, their expressions a mix of determination and apprehension.

"This... This changes everything," Nicky murmured, her eyes darting across the pages. "If we can prove even half of this, it'll be enough to bring down Vince and his cronies."

Gio nodded, his jaw set with resolve. "We need to tread carefully. These people won't hesitate to destroy anyone who threatens their power."

"It's pouring outside. Is Emily still outside?" he asked.

But their conversation was interrupted by the creak of the cabin door, swinging open to reveal a shadowy figure standing on the threshold. Brian's hand instinctively reached for the gun holstered at his side as he squared his shoulders, ready for whatever came next.

"You shouldn't have come here, Giuseppe Rossi," the figure said, their voice low and menacing. "You're playing a dangerous game, and you're outmatched."

Gio's gaze narrowed, his fingers tightening around the file he held. "And who might you be? Another one of Milton's lackeys?"

The figure chuckled darkly, stepping further into the cabin's dim light. "I'm no lackey, Mr. Rossi. I'm someone who knows the truth, someone who understands the stakes."

"Well, then, why don't you step into the light and show yourself?" Gio challenged, his voice steady despite the adrenaline coursing through his veins.

But the figure remained shrouded in darkness, their features obscured by the hood of their cloak. "Some things are better left unseen, Mr. Rossi. Trust me when I say you don't want to know what lies beneath."

Gio's grip tightened even further, his mind racing with possibilities. "I'll take my chances. Now, why don't you tell me what you're doing here… And where's Emily?"

The figure's laughter echoed off the cabin walls, sending shivers down Gio's spine. "You're a brave one; I'll give you that. But bravery won't protect you from what's coming. Don't worry about your little journalist friend; she's just sleeping for a bit. Now, like a good boy, hand over the file, and I'll make sure you see your friend alive."

"How did you find us?" Nicky interjected. As the figure's face turned, Gio, though drenched in sweat, covertly slid the document of Charles's belongings into his pocket.

"I must admit, you are a little good for rookies. But in the end, you are just amateurs," the figure's cackling voice boomed through the cabin.

Infuriated by his words, Brian and Julian aimed their weapons at him when Claire stopped them.

"He has Emily. Don't be reckless."

"Good. Now, be rid of the stubbornness and hand over the file, Mr. Rossi," the figure growled, aiming his gaze at him.

"How do I know that she's alive, or you'll let her go once you have the file?" Gio asked, his heart throbbing wildly with uncertainty.

"That's the game, Mr. Rossi. You don't. Now, then, what will you choose? Your friend or the proof that will damn the ones who oppressed your little beauty," the hooded figure chuckled.

Gio's face turned grim. His mind and heart confiscated into a war—a war of emotions and rationality. As minutes trickled away, his breath turned hefty until Nicky caressed his hand.

"You cannot leave Emily behind. Even if there's a 1% chance of her life being saved, take it," she whispered.

The tension that had woven across Gio's face tethered. Heaving out a sigh, he handed over the file.

"Interesting. I guess you are not as ambitious as I thought. Worry not, we'll meet again soon, I believe. Leave

Ravenbrook while you still can, Mr. Rossi. This is your final warning."

While the hope he had finally seen vanished from his eyes, his heart impaled with the thought of how Vince had checkmated him. Despite the sorrow of loss crippling his strength, Gio stood his ground, his resolve unyielding. "I'm not leaving until I've uncovered the truth, no matter what it takes. I'll make sure the world sees the ugly face you desperately hide,"

With a final, ominous laugh, the figure turned and disappeared into the night, leaving Gio and his team to ponder the gravity of their situation. As the echoes of their encounter faded into the darkness, he couldn't help but feel a sense of foreboding.

He immediately rushed outside to find Emily—she lay unconscious, tied to the tree trunk. Hastily, he checked her pulse—she was alive!

The gamble had paid off, and relief eased the burden everyone felt in their chests. Pushing the the fear of the impending danger that shadowed his comrades' lives aside, he mustered up the strength to fight back, knowing that he couldn't back down now.

With Nicky's love as his guiding light and the truth as his weapon, he would see this through to the end, no matter what challenges lay ahead.

Chapter 13: Echoes of Rain and Justice

Emily woke up in a cold sweat, her breath shaky while her eyes ricocheted from left to right. Her heart raced as the remnants of the pain, the stinging from the sleeping dart injected in the back of her neck, still throbbed. Fear plagued her senses as the whispers of the hooded figure lingered in her mind, "Sleep well."

As her consciousness got entombed in the trauma, Nicky's comforting caressing of her hands and Julian and Claire's smiles of relief lofted Emily out of the state of trauma.

"Are you alright, Emily?" Gio's voice wavered with worry.

"Y-Yeah, I guess," Emily murmured, her voice barely a whisper as she still gathered her senses together.

"Don't worry, we are here with you," Nicky assured her, gently embracing her.

"Thank you... Can you tell me what happened?" Emily asked.

"A lot. We will update you on the way. For now, let's move before someone else ambushes us," Brian alerted from the side as he scoured the surroundings for any intruders.

Emily nodded, taking comfort in their words. Despite her fear, she felt a newfound determination burning within her.

She realized she couldn't let her fear hold her back; she had to fight for justice for herself and all those who had suffered at the hands of the corrupt.

As the predicament of their situation tightened around them, Gio and the others piled into his car while Brian and his squad got into their SUV. Nicky updated Emily on the events that had transpired while she was unconscious. With each detail, her expression changed. The rain beat down on the windshield as they navigated the slick streets of Ravenbrook. Each bead of rain was like an orb of emotions that stormed each of the squad's members, an orb of fear, uncertainty, and an infallible determination.

Meanwhile, Gio contemplated his next step: meeting with Agnes McAllister. Too many questions surrounded her existence as the person who once shone in his eyes like someone who understood justice now seemed like a fraud.

"Hey, Emily. Are you up for the meeting with Agnes?" Gio asked, remembering how invested Emily had been in researching her involvement.

"More than ever. Let's go," her resolve shone through her words.

"Can you please drop me off at the rendezvous point? I need to look into something. Meanwhile, you guys handle Agnes," Nicky chimed in.

Gio's meeting with Agnes McAllister loomed on the horizon, a chance to gather crucial information that could help unravel the mysteries surrounding Milton's organization and the enigma surrounding Agnes that entangled Gio's mind for days. After dropping off Nicky, they approached her mansion. his heart raced with anticipation as he stood in front of the mansion's gate. The time when he first met with Agnes flashed through his mind, but this time, he was in a position where he had the freedom to question her.

Mustering up the courage, refreshing each enigmatic question that Agnes's presence brought forth, Gio rang the doorbell. Agnes, the frail woman who once seemed on the verge of death, now stood adorned in luxurious robes and a lively energy. For a moment, his mind fumbled over the thought of how different she looked.

"Gio, what brings you here today?" Agnes inquired, her voice laced with a hint of frostiness veiled behind a political smile.

"You seem to be doing well, Miss Agnes," Gio greeted.

"Thank you. I indeed do feel well."

"This here is my friend, Emily. We were hoping that we could have a conversation with you, Miss Agnes."

"You have come unannounced, Mr. Rossi. Just like the last time. Would it be—"

"It's just for a moment. We find ourselves at yet another blockade and come seeking your guidance, Miss Agnes," Emily interjected, her voice begging as she realized how Agnes was about to turn them away.

"Just a few moments then. And please, don't interrupt me again," Agnes retorted, a hint of disgust washed over her face.

"That was desperate," Gio whispered to Emily.

"Didn't have a choice. Had to tap into my journalistic instincts," Emily sighed.

"I've been delving into the events surrounding Charles Blackwood's demise," Gio began cautiously, observing Agnes's reaction closely. "The bloodstained curtains in his mansion, the rumors swirling around town... It all paints a rather intriguing picture."

Agnes's lips tightened imperceptibly, her gaze flickering away for a moment before she met Gio's eyes once more. "I'm sure you're aware that Charles and I were not exactly on the best of terms," she replied tersely. "But whatever happened to him, it was his own doing."

Gio nodded, though his mind buzzed with questions. If Agnes truly despised Charles, why would she continue to associate herself with him, especially if he was involved in illicit activities?

"And what about the courtroom drama between Milton and yourself, Mrs. McAllister?" Gio pressed, carefully gauging Agnes's reaction. "It's rather unusual for two such prominent figures in Ravenbrook to have such a public falling out."

Agnes's jaw tightened visibly, a flicker of something

unreadable passing through her eyes. "Milton and I had our differences, yes," she admitted, her tone guarded. "But he was always a friend of the family. Whatever disagreements we had, they were...personal."

Gio's mind raced with speculation. If Agnes and Milton were once allies, what could have driven them apart? And more importantly, what role did Agnes play in Milton's organization, if any?

As the conversation continued, Gio probed delicately, each question a carefully crafted attempt to unravel the truth without arousing suspicion. And with each carefully chosen word, he couldn't shake the feeling that Agnes was hiding something, something that could hold the key to unlocking the mysteries of Ravenbrook's dark underbelly.

Agnes shifted uncomfortably in her seat, her gaze flickering towards the rain-drenched window before returning to meet Gio's probing stare. "You see, Mr. Rossi, Ravenbrook is not as idyllic as it may seem on the surface," she began, her voice tinged with resignation. "There are forces at play here that go beyond the scope of mere family disputes."

Gio leaned in, his interest piqued. "Forces? What kind of forces, Mrs. McAllister?"

Agnes sighed as if steeling herself to reveal long-held secrets. "Power, Mr. Rossi. The kind of power that can make or break a person's reputation, that can dictate the course of entire lives," she explained cryptically. "And in a town like

Ravenbrook, where old money and influence reign supreme, one must tread carefully if they wish to survive."

Gio's mind raced as he processed Agnes's words. So, it wasn't just personal animosity that drove her involvement with Milton; it was a tangled web of power and influence, a world where alliances shifted like sand in the wind.

"And what about your dealings with Milton's organization?" Gio pressed, his tone gentle yet insistent. "Surely there must be more to your involvement than meets the eye."

Agnes hesitated, her gaze flickering away for a moment before she met Gio's eyes once more, her expression guarded yet strangely vulnerable.

"I did what I had to do to protect my family, Mr. Rossi," she confessed, her voice barely above a whisper. "In a town like Ravenbrook, sometimes one must make... compromises in order to survive."

Gio's heart sank as he realized the depth of Agnes's involvement with Milton's organization. She was not just a bystander caught in the crossfire; she was a player in the game, willing to do whatever it took to safeguard her family's interests, even if it meant dancing with the devil himself.

As the rain continued to drum against the windowpane, he couldn't shake the feeling that he was teetering on the edge of a precipice, one wrong move away from plunging into the abyss of Ravenbrook's darkest secrets. But he was determined to see this through, to uncover the truth no matter the cost, for the sake of Nicky, for the sake of justice.

Later that evening, Gio and the others gathered in their makeshift headquarters, poring over evidence and material for initiating a trial against General Cole. Maps, documents, and witness statements littered the table as they worked tirelessly into the night, determined to bring the corrupt to justice.

Seated around the dimly lit table, the soft glow of the overhead lamp casting long shadows across the room, Gio, Emily, Nicky, and Keisuke huddled together, their faces illuminated by the glow of their laptops as they poured over stacks of documents and digital files.

"Alright, let's review what we've got so far," Gio began, his voice firm with determination. "Emily, you've been digging into General Cole's military record, right?"

Emily nodded, her fingers flying across the keyboard as she pulled up various documents on her laptop screen. "Yes, I've been going through his service history, looking for any signs of misconduct or corruption," she replied. "So far, I've found several instances where his actions were... questionable, to say the least."

Gio leaned in, his eyes narrowing as he studied the information displayed on Emily's screen. "Such as?"

"Instances of bribery, coercion, even allegations of war crimes," Emily listed off, her voice tinged with disgust. "It seems General Cole has a long history of bending the rules to suit his own agenda."

Nicky chimed in, her fingers tapping away at her own laptop keyboard as she cross-referenced information with Emily's findings. "And let's not forget his connections to Milton," she added, her voice tight with barely concealed anger. "There are records of meetings between the two of them dating back years, long before any of this came to light."

Gio nodded grimly, his mind racing as he processed the implications of their discoveries. "So, it's safe to say that General Cole is not exactly a model citizen," he concluded, his tone heavy with sarcasm.

Keisuke interjected, his voice soft yet filled with determination. "And what about his financial records? Have we found anything linking him to Milton's organization?"

Nicky shook her head, the frustration evident in her expression. "Not yet. But I'm still digging. With Keisuke's help, we should be able to uncover something soon."

Gio glanced around the table, his gaze meeting each of his team members' eyes in turn. "Alright, let's keep at it. We need to gather as much evidence as possible before we make our move against General Cole," he instructed, his voice firm with resolve.

With the rain still pounding against the windows, the team's efforts intensified. Emily and Gio sifted through the hard copies of documents, their eyes scanning each page for any shred of evidence that could further incriminate General Cole. Meanwhile, Keisuke worked his magic on his laptop, his fingers flying across the keyboard as he accessed Milton's personal records from the military website.

"Got it!" Keisuke exclaimed, a triumphant grin spreading across his face as he uncovered a treasure trove of information buried within Milton's files. "There's a whole section here detailing his connections to various high-ranking officials, including General Cole."

Gio and Emily exchanged a look of excitement and disbelief. "This is it," Gio breathed, his heart pounding with anticipation. "With this evidence, we'll finally be able to take down General Cole and expose Milton's network for what it really is."

Emily nodded, her eyes shining with determination. "Let's get to work," she declared, her voice filled with conviction.

As Gio, Emily, Nicky, and Keisuke meticulously combed through the evidence, they realized a glaring gap in their findings: there was nothing directly tying General Cole to the murder of Jeremy Denver. Frustration simmered beneath the surface as they confronted this obstacle.

"We have everything we need to prove Cole's corruption and involvement with Milton, but without concrete evidence of his direct involvement in Jeremy's murder, our case may not hold up in court," Emily lamented, her brow furrowed with concern.

Gio nodded thoughtfully, his mind racing with possibilities. "We need to find a way to connect the dots," he mused, his voice tinged with determination. "We know Cole's methods, his modus operandi. If we can gather evidence that links him to Jeremy's murder, we'll have everything we need to bring him down."

Nicky's eyes gleamed with newfound determination. "What if we go back to the scene of the crime? Maybe there's something we missed, some clue that could lead us to the truth," she suggested, her voice brimming with hope.

Gio nodded in agreement. "It's worth a shot," he replied, his mind already racing ahead to formulate a plan. "We'll revisit the mill where Jeremy's body was found. Maybe there's something there that we overlooked."

Keisuke chimed in, his voice filled with excitement. "And while we're there, I can use my skills to hack into the security cameras in the area. If there's any footage of Cole or his associates near the scene of the crime, we'll find it," he offered, his fingers itching to get to work.

With a renewed sense of purpose, the team set their plan into motion. They knew that their journey was far from over, but with their determination and resourcefulness, they were confident that they would uncover the truth and bring General Cole to justice.

For hours on end, they poured over the newly uncovered information, piecing together the puzzle of General Cole's corruption and involvement in Milton's organization. Each document and piece of evidence brought them one step closer to their goal.

As they stood together, their hands trembling with anticipation, Gio and Emily exchanged a look of triumph. "We did it," Emily whispered, her voice filled with awe and wonder.

Gio smiled, a sense of pride swelling within him. "Yes, we did," he agreed, his heart swelling with gratitude for the team that had stood by his side through it all, "Just one last piece left, and we can imprison him for life."

With their evidence prepared and their resolve unwavering, they knew that they were ready to take on whatever challenges lay ahead. And as they prepared to present their case in court, they knew that justice would finally be served—at least they hoped for it.

As the rain continued to drum against the windows, casting a somber pall over the room, Gio couldn't shake the feeling that they were closing in on their target, that the pieces of the puzzle were finally starting to fall into place.

Despite the dangers that lay ahead, Gio knew that they couldn't afford to back down. They had come too far to turn back now, and with each piece of evidence they uncovered, their resolve only strengthened. Despite the storm raging outside, Gio and his team were prepared to deal with any challenges that came their way.

Chapter 14: Blood Stains and Broken Codes

It was late after midnight as Gio, Nicky, Emily, and Keisuke made their way towards the old mill. The hope of finding the breakthrough they needed in their case flickered. The possibility of being ambushed at the mill clouded their senses with fear as the distance to the mill shortened with each passing minute.

The storm clouds, veiling the moon, mirrored the turmoil brewing inside each of their hearts. The chill in the air, the overcast weather's murkiness, and the thunder's low rumbling—each element intensified the dangers lurking in the depths of the darkness.

However, amidst the fog of these depressing emotions, their purpose remained vivid and clear—manifesting as the courage they needed in such times. As they neared the mill, Emily broke the silence.

"We are going, but what if there are guards like before, Gio? Snipers. Do we have a plan for how to bypass them?"

"Unlikely. After Jeremy's corpse was found there, I doubt they would draw any more attention to themselves in that manner," Gio concluded as he parked the car in front of the 'Private property' signboard. "If there are any, then we'll adapt."

"Adapt? What do you mean to adapt?" Emily muttered in a low voice. "We aren't fighters or anything, Gio."

"You overlooked one thing, Emily. We have critical thinking, which, at times, can be more powerful than a gun," he smirked as he got out of the car.

Scoffing, Emily followed suit, as did Nicky and Keisuke. Striding through the thick foliage surrounding the mill, taking each step with caution imbued in them, the squad made their way to an altitude and searched the surroundings of the mill for any guards.

"I don't see any," said Keisuke as he adjusted his backpack.

"Neither do I. It's quiet. Strangely quiet," Nicky added.

"It may be strange, but it's in our best interests. If things go wrong, we'll figure it out," said Gio, his eyes darting from East to West. "Let's go."

"Let's hope everything goes well," Emily whispered, her head throbbing with the memories of how the hooded figure had knocked her out in Charles's cabin.

Thunder cracked in the distance, and rain cascaded down in unrelenting sheets, drowning out any sound beyond the old mill. Inside, the dim light flickered from a single bulb, casting long shadows across the cold industrial space where Gio, Emily, Nicky, and Keisuke stood, their breaths held in uneasy anticipation. They had come to the place where Jeremy Denver's body had been found, hoping for answers to be hidden in the smeared blood marks across the floor.

But the air inside felt oppressive, as if the walls

themselves held secrets too dangerous to reveal. Gio's imagination ran rampant—each piece of his thought aligning to form the image of the night he and Emily witnessed the cult's gathering outside the mill, imagining the kind of atrocities they would have planned and committed within these walls.

'Only if walls could voice what they heard,' he thought to himself.

"This place seems too…miserable," said Emily, her voice barely audible over the pattering of the rain as she stood beside Gio. Her eyes ricocheted from one crevice to another as she gauged the dilapidated mill, the cracks in the walls, and the rusty machinery imbuing the atmosphere with an eerie, forgotten feel—a place perfect for evil whom they were chasing.

"Not really a surprise," Gio replied, his voice steady but low, his eyes fixed on the far end of the mill that opened up to the creek, where Jeremy's body had been discovered.

The weight of the place pressed down on him, and despite the cold, sweat beaded on the back of his neck. They were getting closer, but with each step, the danger seemed to multiply. "There's little time to waste. Keisuke, check the CCTV (Closed-Circuit Television). Nicky, keep watch around the perimeter while Emily and I will search the premises for any clues."

"Already on it," Keisuke replied, his fingers flying over the keyboard as he hacked into the CCTV's database.

In an instant, each person took their spots as they were assigned. The clock continued to tick until Keisuke's voice alerted everyone.

"I found something!" He yelled.

Gio stood over Keisuke's shoulder, watching the grainy footage of a figure slipping into the mill on the night of Jeremy Denver's murder. The timestamp confirmed their worst suspicions. Whoever this was, they had moved with cold precision, disappearing into the building mere hours before Jeremy's body was found.

"Pause it," Gio said, tension tight in his voice. "Zoom in on their face."

Keisuke did his best to enhance the image, but the figure's hood was pulled low, masking their features. Still, something about the way they moved—it wasn't just professional. It was predatory, something that resonated deeply with the hooded figure in Gio's mind.

"You recognize anything?" Emily whispered, her eyes locked on the screen.

"I'm not sure," Gio said, his stomach twisting. "But whoever this is, they're not someone who makes mistakes… like him."

"Him?" Emily asked.

"I'm sure it's the same person who followed us to that cabin. Who followed me since the day of Nicky's trial," said Gio, his voice laced with dread and something close to anger.

Suddenly, Keisuke froze, his eyes locked on something else on the screen—a terminal, visible for just a second behind the figure as they slipped into the mill. "Wait," Keisuke said, his voice barely above a whisper. "That's not just some old terminal. That's connected to a hidden network of wires—right there. I didn't notice it before because it's practically camouflaged in dust and debris. We might be able to get something off it—something that wasn't scrubbed from the servers if I'm able to connect to it. Hoping against hope, it's still in the working phase."

Before anyone could respond, the creak of a door echoed from the far end of the mill—the metal hinges of the door scratching against the floor, filling the air with a sharp screeching noise. The hairs on the back of Gio's neck stood. A shiver of cold ran down each person's spine. Keisuke froze in his place as he was checking the terminal. Emily's face turned pale, and Nicky's hand slid toward the concealed gun in her jacket, though she hadn't pulled it just yet.

They weren't alone.

Nicky's eyes scanned the darkness beyond them. "Who's there?" she called out, seeing there was no place to hide nearby in time, and the encounter was inevitable. Her voice remained remarkably steady despite the hammering of her heart.

Only silence resounded from the other end. The footsteps grew louder, heavier. The figure from the video appeared from the shadows at the edge of the room, tall and broad, their face hidden beneath the hood of a coat. Gio's hands were clenched, his nails pierced into his skin, and his eyes were glaring at the hooded figure—it was him.

He knew that devilish aura surrounding the figure. The hooded man moved with the same cold efficiency as in the footage—like someone who knew they were in control.

Gio's heart raced as the figure stepped closer. His mind scrambled to understand what they were up against, but he was out of his depth. For a split second, no one spoke. The storm outside was the only sound; its fury was a mere breeze compared to the tension building inside.

"You're in over your head, Mr. Rossi," the figure said, their voice a low growl, dripping with confidence. "Turn back now before you regret it. You have come far too near your death."

Gio forced himself to breathe, but his pulse throbbed in his ears. His eyes darted towards Nicky—he could feel the fear seeping through her bones, but her steadfast gaze filled his heart with courage. He realized that although he had dealt with plenty of dangerous people in courtrooms, this wasn't a courtroom. This was a fight for survival.

Still, he had one weapon—the only one he was good at using: words, and he could distract the figure so that Nicky and others could find their way out.

"And what exactly am I regretting?" Gio asked, stepping forward, keeping his movements slow, non-threatening, gulping the coldness of fear crawling up his throat. His eyes remained locked on the shadowed face, searching for any sign of hesitation—any hint of a recognizable face. "Trying to uncover the truth? Or is it the fact that we've gotten too close?"

The man didn't flinch. His hands remained clasped behind his back while he slowly strode back and forth horizontally.

"I told you we will meet again, Mr. Rossi. Fate has bound us together," the hoarse voice echoed again. "Isn't it fated— You, gasping for justice, and me, straggling the very thing you seek?" He laughed, throwing his hands to the sides.

"Fated, you say? I think it is fate taking its course towards what you seem to be hellbent on straggling," Gio chuckled, slowly approaching the hooded figure. "What's fate is that justice never chokes. In the end, it only prevails, whether it be after a decade or tomorrow. It'll find its way. I think that's fated."

"We all have one foot in the fairytale and one in the abyss, Mr. Rossi. Your fairytale is about seeking justice in this corrupt world. I wonder where your abyss lies… Perhaps, in the very love you so earnestly protect," the hooded figure snickered as his footsteps came to a halt, just a breath away from Gio. Even under the hood, his face remained veiled by a mask, but his eyes—those emotionless eyes, struck Gio with a realization that he hadn't thought of before.

"If it's such a fairytale, then why do you so dearly protect it? A fable is a fable, after all. No one would believe it even if we told it," Gio quipped, barely keeping his senses together.

Glaring into Gio's eyes, the man remained silent. Instead, he reached into his coat and pulled out a sleek, black handgun, the barrel gleaming in the dim light.

"I fear I have gotten bored of your nonsensical chatter, Mr. Rossi."

Emily gasped and took a step back. Keisuke's hands froze, hovering over his laptop.

Gio took another step forward, his mind racing as he tried to stay calm. This man wasn't here to scare them—he was here to make sure they didn't leave with what they'd found. But Gio had to buy time.

"You think pulling that gun solves anything?" Gio asked, his voice calm but tight. "Shoot me, and what? Your problems get worse. We already know too much."

The figure tilted his head slightly, the barrel still aimed at Gio's chest. His movements were measured—controlled, like a predator waiting for the right moment to strike.

"You're not as clever as you think, Mr. Rossi," the man said, his voice cold and calculated. He shifted his grip on the gun, and before Gio could react, he moved. The man lunged, his hand shooting out with terrifying speed, slamming into Gio's chest with a brutal punch.

The force knocked the wind out of his lungs. He stumbled backward, gasping for air. His vision blurred as he hit the cold concrete floor. Pain exploded across his back and ribs, and he struggled to regain his bearings.

The man was on him in an instant, pinning him to the ground amidst the shrieks of Emily and Nicky while Keisuke, finding the opportunity, continued with establishing the connection with the terminal—his hands quivering with fear, eyebrows beaded with sweat, but he continued. With terrifying precision, the man grabbed Gio by the collar, yanking him up with one hand and slamming him back down.

"You talk too much, but that's common for your kind," the man growled, leaning closer as he tightened his grip on Gio's shirt. "Maybe I'll rip that sugary tongue of yours first."

From the corner of his eye, Gio saw Nicky reach for her gun.

"Stop!" Nicky's voice rang out, sharp and commanding. Her gun was aimed directly at the back of the man's head, her hands trembling, but her resolve unwavering as tears shone in her eyes, seeing Gio wince in pain.

The man didn't flinch. Instead, he slowly released his grip on Gio and stood, his cold eyes locking on Nicky. His demeanor never changed—he was still in control, even with a gun pointed at him.

"You won't shoot me, Nicky," he said, his voice chillingly calm as he took a slow step toward her. "Behind this strong woman act is just an empty shell, void of any willpower to kill someone."

Nicky's hands trembled, but she didn't back down. "Try me," she whispered, the barrel of her gun following his every move.

The man's eyes flicked to Gio, lying on the floor, struggling to get up. "You should've stayed out of this, Mr. Rossi," he said, his tone darker now. "But you're too late. Jeremy's dead because he couldn't keep his mouth shut, and tonight was your turn. However, it seems fate has sided with you once again this time."

The words hit like a sledgehammer. Jeremy's murder hadn't been a random act—it was deliberate—a calculated move. Gio struggled to his feet, blood pounding in his ears as he realized the weight of what lay beneath this murder.

"So it was you," Gio managed to rasp, clutching his side in pain. "You killed him."

The man's lips curled into a cruel smile. "Let's just say he knew too much." His eyes flicked to Nicky, then to the laptop still on Keisuke's desk. "And now, so do you."

Before anyone could react, the man took a swift step backward, disappearing into the shadows as easily as he had appeared. The rain roared louder, masking his retreat, and just like that—he was gone, with his last words fading along with him, "Luck won't side with you next time."

For a long moment, no one moved. Nicky's hands were still shaking, the gun held in front of her as if she hadn't yet processed that the immediate danger had passed. Emily let out a shaky breath, her heart hammering in her chest.

Keisuke, meanwhile, sat frozen, his fingers hovering over the keyboard as the screen in front of him revealed something they hadn't expected. "Gio... Look at this," Keisuke whispered, his voice trembling with disbelief and relief that they won't die tonight at least.

Gio limped over, his ribs screaming in pain with every step, but what he saw on the screen made his blood run cold. Keisuke had cracked into the mill's hidden network, and what they found was more than just military records—it was a ledger of payments, transfers, and a list of names marked for elimination.

Jeremy Denver's name was there, crossed out along with many other names.

But it wasn't just Jeremy. As they traced down the names, there was another crossed name: *Charles Blackwood.*

For a moment, Nicky and Gio's hearts drowned in silence—proof of their doubts thumping their brains. Someone from within the organization got Charles murdered. Other names followed; some they recognized, and some they didn't. And at the very bottom, underlined in red, were two more names that turned Gio's stomach.

Nicoletta Bianchi.

Giuseppe Rossi.

"We're on the list," Gio whispered, his voice barely audible.

Nicky's breath hitched, and her face paled as she stared

at the screen. They had uncovered more than they had bargained for—Jeremy had been silenced for getting too close, Charles was assassinated for power or the reason they didn't know yet, and now they were next.

"We need to get out of here," Gio said, urgency thick in his voice. "They know we're here. We've got what we need, but we have to move. Now!"

As they hurried out of the mill and into the storm, the weight of their discovery hung over them like a death sentence. Jeremy's killer had slipped through their fingers, but the truth was now in their hands. They had the evidence to bring Milton and General Cole's network to its knees, but with every step closer to the truth, they were one step closer to being hunted themselves. The stakes had risen, the cost heavy, and justice still far from sight.

Chapter 15: Tipping the Scales

The rain had eased to a slow drizzle by the time Gio and his team regrouped in the dimly lit hideout along the borders of Ravenbrook. The storm outside may have calmed, but inside, the tension was palpable—the last encounter etched deep into their mind. After a long and mentally exhausting journey back home—death hung upon their shoulders at each turn—they could finally breathe.

"I never thought I would come to like this abode, but it seems like heaven right now," Emily huffed as she slumped onto the couch.

"Tell me about it," Nicky added as she poured some wine for herself.

"Come on, guys. No time to waste," Gio said, clapping his hands. "Keisuke, round everyone up. We are having a meeting right now."

As everyone gathered around the dinner table, the air thickened with the weight of the evidence they had uncovered, the revelations they had stumbled upon, and the growing sense of danger that seemed to loom closer with every step they took forward.

Gio sat at the head of the table, his ribs still aching from the encounter with the hooded figure at the mill. His fingers drummed lightly on the surface as he stared down at the scattered documents, photos, and digital files—the ones Keisuke mined from the mill's terminal—splayed across the table. The evidence was damning, but assembling it all into a cohesive case—one strong enough to take down someone as powerful as General Cole—felt like an impossible task.

Emily was the first to break the silence. "So... This is it?" she asked, her voice low but firm. "This is everything we have on General Cole."

Keisuke nodded, scrolling through the digital files on his laptop. "We've pieced together everything we've gathered. The financial records, the transaction logs, and the list of targets. It's all here." He tapped a few keys, and a series of documents appeared on the screen—each one more incriminating than the last. "This shows Cole's connections to Milton's organization. The payments, the off-the-record meetings, everything that ties him to this mess."

Nicky, seated to the side, leaned forward. Her hands, still trembling slightly from the earlier encounter, clenched into fists. "And what about Jeremy? We know Cole had him killed, but we need to make that stick in court. Without direct evidence, they'll dismiss it as circumstantial."

Gio inhaled deeply, the sharp pain in his ribs reminding him just how close they had come to losing everything. He leaned back, letting his eyes drift over the team, each member reflecting a different kind of exhaustion. But they couldn't stop. Not now.

"Let's go through it all again," he said quietly, rubbing his temple. "We need to make sure we haven't missed anything. Remember, right now, our target is Cole. We'll get the bigger fish one by one. Even though Milton gave Cole up, bringing things to the court and presenting a solid case will put pressure on the others. And under pressure, even the slickest slip and fall sometimes."

"What if they go into hiding afterward?" Claire asked.

"They might, and if they do, that means it worked. No evil can lurk in silence for too long. They'll eventually make their move, and we'll be there to catch them when they do," Brian added as he chewed through his steak.

"Brian's right. Instead of being on the defensive, we should be offensive and see where that takes us," Gio agreed.

As everyone nodded in acknowledgment of the plan, they sifted through the evidence. The team revisited every key moment that had led them to where they stood now—every dangerous encounter, every cryptic lead.

Emily pulled up the first file, her fingers tracing over a report as she spoke. "It all started with the money laundering link we found regarding Agnes and Milton. We knew Cole was involved with something bigger, something dangerous behind the scenes, after further expanding on the case. But it wasn't until we found out about his connection to Milton that we realized how deep this went."

Nicky added, "Then there was the confrontation with Milton's men at the old factory. That's when we found the first real piece of evidence linking Cole to the Disciples—those encrypted emails. Before, we only knew he was close with Wagner as per his description in his autobiography."

She flipped through her notes. "It was subtle at first. Just small mentions of a *higher authority* involved in their operations. But when we decrypted the files, Cole's name came up. That's when we knew."

Gio jumped in, his voice tense. "Then there was the incident of my meeting with Milton. When I probed closer to the subject of assassination, Milton's answer indicated something big that was about to go down."

The room grew quieter as they recalled the murder at the mill. Gio's voice was low as he spoke. "When that man left Jeremy's body at the mill, that was the final nail in the coffin. It wasn't just about eliminating Jeremy anymore. It was about sending a message. And we all know who that message was meant for—us."

Gio's eyes darkened as he looked at the evidence they'd built, each step bringing them closer to uncovering General Cole's true role in the conspiracy. Every encounter, every fight, every risk they'd taken had brought them to this moment.

With the evidence laid out, it was time to discuss how they would use it to bring down Cole. Gio stood, wincing slightly from the pain in his side, and began pacing slowly around the room. "Here's how we're going to do it," he said, his voice measured and deliberate.

"First, we hit Cole with the financial records." Gio gestured toward the files on the screen.

"These payments from Milton's organization tie directly

back to Cole's offshore accounts. We've traced the funds, thanks to Claire and the team, and it's clear that Cole was profiting from illegal deals with Milton. The transfers were disguised as military contracts, but we have the transaction logs that show otherwise."

Keisuke nodded, scrolling through the files. "And we can prove that Cole used his military connections to shield Milton's operations. He provided security clearances, access to classified intel, and even used his influence to silence whistleblowers—like Jeremy."

Emily chimed in, "But we need more than just the financials. We need to make it personal. That's where Jeremy's murder comes in."

Gio turned to face them, his expression grim. "We know Cole ordered the hit on Jeremy, but we need to connect the dots in court. We don't have much in that regard other than Milton's words that Cole ordered the hit. Then there's that man's words—it's vague, but he all but confirmed that Jeremy was silenced because he knew too much."

"We still don't have a motive that connects Cole to the murder, Gio," Nicky added.

Gio clenched his fists. "We pincer Cole with the financials, and while he's distracted by all that, Nicky and her team will be finding that motive. Does that work?" Gio asked, meeting Nicky and her team's gaze.

"I'm sure we can find something," Claire added.

"It'll be a race against time, and we would need that evidence to get Cole the sentence he truly deserves," Gio's brows knitted together as he remembered the atrocities he had aided Milton and others in.

"So, to grasp a better judgment of how much time you guys will have, I'll explain how we'll begin the case. We'll start with the evidence of his illegal dealings with Milton—play around with hypothetical questions and theories to keep them occupied and stall the trial as long as we can. Meanwhile, Emily, you'll dig up every rumor and every piece of conspiracy theory and anything that could be used against Cole. Once the court sees that Cole had both the means and the motive, it'll be impossible for him to worm his way out."

"That's all good, but why are we rushing this all of a sudden? We can bring things to trial after we have evidence of Cole's involvement in the murder," Emily pondered out loud.

"Because we are out of time, Emily. With our names on the hitlist and them breathing this close to our necks, we can't move forward unless we fight back a little. Distract them," Gio answered. "I'm afraid that was our last warning, and I can't risk all of your lives again like that. I'll put up a fight at my own battleground and keep them distracted while you guys can search for evidence more freely."

"I think it's a better option. This will give us more room to investigate properly," Julian acknowledged.

But as they spoke, the unspoken fear lingered in the air. They all knew what was coming. Milton wasn't going to sit by and let one of his key allies be taken down. Even though he had ratted out Cole himself, he would react when things spiraled a little out of his expectations. The Disciples—especially someone like Wagner—would retaliate the moment the case hit the courtroom, considering how close he seemed to be with Cole unless it was just Cole admiring him.

Emily's voice was barely above a whisper as she voiced what everyone had been thinking. "Once we file this lawsuit, Milton and the others will come after us. They'll do everything they can to bury this case. Maybe even bury us."

Keisuke, usually the most optimistic of the group, looked grim as he tapped at his laptop. "They have the resources. If they want to make us disappear, they can. Hell, we've already seen how easy it was for them to eliminate Jeremy and track us to the mill."

Nicky crossed her arms, her jaw tight. "We knew the risks when we started this. And we've come too far to turn back now."

Gio nodded, his eyes hard with determination. "We're not turning back. But we need to be prepared. Once this lawsuit is filed, we're targets. Milton and his Disciples will act, but I'll be their center of attention, not you guys. I'll try to take things slow to avoid offending them too quickly so you guys can have ample time to dig deeper. Maybe not directly—at first—but they'll try to discredit us, sabotage our evidence, or do anything to stop this case from going to trial once they realize they are linked with Cole's embezzlements, too. We have to be ready for that."

The weight of his words hung in the air. They had built their case, but the fight was far from over. Now, they were going to war, and their enemies wouldn't be playing by the same rules as they had been until now.

As the clock ticked toward dawn, the team worked tirelessly, reviewing every piece of evidence and every legal maneuver they would use against General Cole. The plan was clear. First, they would file the lawsuit in federal court, using the financial evidence to establish a pattern of illegal dealings between Cole and Milton. From there, they would introduce the evidence tying Cole to Jeremy's murder—building a case so airtight that even Cole's influence couldn't suppress it.

"We're going to use the media, too," Emily said, her voice steady as she glanced toward Gio. "Once we file, we leak the story to the press. The public needs to know what kind of man Cole really is, and guys at media can create one good distraction. That'll make it harder for Milton to make this all disappear when things start spinning out of his control."

Gio nodded in agreement. "Good. We'll use the court of public opinion. Once people see the truth, it'll be harder for them to ignore it. But we need to be careful. If we tip our hand too early, they might try to silence us before we even get to court."

The pressure weighed on all of them, but Gio felt it most. His mind raced through the upcoming legal battle and the countless ways it could go wrong. But failure wasn't an option. Too much was at stake.

The rain had finally stopped when they packed up their files, gathered their bags, and prepared for the next step—the courthouse.

Gio paused at the door, looking back at his team. Their faces were tired, but their resolve was clear. This was it. The culmination of everything they had fought for—a new beginning to the fight that had been going on for far too long behind the curtains.

He took a deep breath, the cold morning air filling his lungs. "Let's go," he said quietly. "It's time."

With that, they stepped into the dawn, their path uncertain but their mission clear.

Chapter 16: The Crossroads

The warmth of the morning sun breezed through the town, diffusing through the gray clouds and casting a muted light over the drenched streets of Ravenbrook. Gio and Emily moved quickly, side by side, heading toward the courthouse. Nicky and the others had already dispersed to gather more evidence, working separately to avoid attracting attention. This morning's mission was clear: file the lawsuit and put the first nail in General Cole's coffin.

Gio's breath fogged in the cold air, his thoughts sharp and focused despite the constant buzz of adrenaline. Emily, walking beside him, mirrored his tension, though her face remained calm—her mind clouded with the thoughts of how things would spiral out once the lawsuit gets filed. The courthouse was only a few blocks away, but every step felt heavier, as though the weight of what they were about to do pressed down on them.

"Once we file this," Emily said quietly, "it's out of our hands."

"I know," Gio replied, his voice clipped. "But if we proceed as planned, it won't get out of hand. We've been preparing for this. No turning back now."

As they reached the courthouse steps, something felt off. Gio hesitated, scanning the building's exterior. It was too quiet. No one was around, no usual bustle of people, and the few security guards present were standing stiffly at the entrance, eyes scanning the area. He had been here a lot, but this was the first time a sense of eeriness crawled under his skin—his instincts throbbed with warning that something was off.

Emily noticed it, too. "Do you think Cole's already making his move?"

"He's too smart to sit back," Gio said. "But we're ready for this. I'm just curious as to how he knew of our plan…"

Dissuading the nagging thoughts, they pushed forward, climbing the stone steps and stepping inside. The atmosphere inside the courthouse was eerily formal, more than usual, with clerks huddled in small groups, whispering in low voices. Something was wrong. Gulping, Gio scanned the interior—curious yet reluctant to find out what moves Cole played or if it was Milton's doing.

At the clerk's desk, a young woman glanced nervously at the documents Gio handed her. "I-I'm sorry, Mr. Rossi," she said, her voice shaking slightly. "There's been a hold on all cases related to General Cole. We've received a directive."

Gio's pulse spiked, but he kept his expression neutral. "A directive? From whom?"

The clerk swallowed, clearly uncomfortable. "It came down from higher up. We can't accept any filings related to military personnel until further notice."

Emily's eyes widened, and she looked at Gio, waiting for his reaction. Cole had anticipated their move, and this wasn't a minor complication. He had somehow managed to leverage his influence to stall the legal process. If the lawsuit couldn't be filed, their entire strategy would crumble before it even started.

Gio, however, didn't panic. His head ached with a rush of countless thoughts, but he remained purposeful—he wouldn't let Cole beat him in his own domain. He leaned forward slightly, keeping his tone measured but firm. "We have known each other for a long time, Gloria. You know as well as I do that what you're describing is highly irregular. There's no law that grants such blanket protection to military personnel, not without formal orders. Show me the directive."

The clerk, Gloria, shifted uncomfortably. "I don't have it here. It's..."

"Then it's not official," Gio interrupted, his voice steady but authoritative. "What you're doing right now is obstructing legal proceedings. If there's no written directive in place, you're required by law to accept this filing. And if you don't, I'll make sure that becomes a separate case all on its own—one that involves civil rights violations and legal obstruction."

Gloria's face paled, and she glanced nervously at a senior clerk behind her, who was pretending to be busy with paperwork. "I... I need to speak with my supervisor."

"Go ahead," Gio said, his confidence unwavering. "But I suggest you hurry. Every minute you delay this filing is another minute the culprits have to maneuver things in their favor. We'll make sure the court knows that, too."

The clerk practically sprinted to the back office, leaving Gio and Emily standing at the counter. Emily exhaled softly, glancing at Gio. "That was impressive."

Gio didn't respond right away. His mind was racing through legal contingencies, planning their next steps if this gambit didn't work. He knew Cole's reach extended deep into the system, but there were limits, and Gio would push those limits as far as they would go.

The senior clerk, a middle-aged man with thinning hair, approached the counter, looking irritable. "Mr. Rossi, you're causing a disruption. I understand you're trying to file an urgent case, but there are sensitive issues involved."

Gio gave the man a cold smile. "Sly old man," Gio muttered under his breath. The clerk's brows twitched. Coughing, Gio continued, "I'm aware. I'm also aware that this court has no legal grounds to refuse the filing unless you have a court order in hand. And from what I can see, you don't."

The senior clerk hesitated, clearly weighing his options. He knew the law just as well as Gio did, and he knew Gio was right. Finally, after a tense pause, he sighed. "Fine. We'll process the filing, but don't expect this to be easy, Mr. Rossi. There will be delays."

"I'm used to delays," Gio said smoothly, his gaze never wavering. "But you should be prepared for more if this filing doesn't go through today."

With a resigned look, the clerk took the documents and began processing them. Emily let out a quiet breath of relief as the papers were finally stamped, and their lawsuit was officially filed.

As they turned to leave, Emily glanced at Gio. "That was too close."

Gio nodded, his expression serious. "Cole's already moving pieces. This is just the beginning."

They stepped back out into the cold morning air, but the tension hadn't lifted. If anything, it had deepened. Straightening his crimson tie that complimented his jet-black blazer, Gio thought to himself, *'Filing the lawsuit had been the first step, but Cole's reach was already showing. He had the power to stall, to complicate, and to twist the system in his favor. I have managed to outmaneuver him this time, but let's see where this heads. No going back now.'*

"We need to move fast," Gio said as they headed toward the car. "Nicky and the others need more time to find solid evidence linking Cole to Jeremy's murder. Without that, we won't have enough to pin him down for good. And now that the lawsuit is in the system, he'll be watching every move we make."

Emily nodded, pulling out her phone. "I'll check in with Nicky and see how they're progressing. We can't afford any slip-ups now."

As they drove away from the courthouse, the pressure weighed heavier on them. They had won a small victory, but Gio knew Cole wouldn't stay quiet for long. The system was rigged in Cole's favor, and now they were playing a dangerous game. If they made even one mistake, everything would come crashing down.

Gio's phone buzzed in his pocket again. Another message from one of his sources in the courthouse: "Cole knows you filed."

Gio clenched his jaw, his mind already working on their next move. They were being watched, and Cole must be preparing to strike. But so was Gio. He had spent years navigating corrupt systems, defending clients against impossible odds.

This time, he wasn't just defending someone—he was attacking. And he wasn't going to let General Cole slip away.

He turned to Emily as they drove. "Cole knows we've got the lawsuit in. We're going to have to be smarter and faster. Cole's going to try everything to shut us down."

Emily's eyes met his, steely and determined. "Then we hit back twice as hard. I'll leak pieces of information to the media, put pressure on him from there."

Gio nodded. "Do that. We need to pincer attack him, restrain him from pulling any brazen moves."

With that, they drove toward the next phase of their plan,

ready to fight every step of the way.

Meanwhile, on the other side, Nicky crouched behind a rusted dumpster in a narrow alley, her phone vibrating in her pocket. She glanced down, the message from Emily flashing on her screen: "Lawsuit filed. Ran into trouble, but Gio handled it. Be careful."

Nicky exhaled softly, her breath visible in the cold morning air. "Handled it" meant Gio had likely faced more complications than Emily was letting on, but at least the first step was done. Now, it was her turn. Along with her team, Nicky had ventured towards one of the old warehouses Charles frequented. *'I hope you hid something here, Charles.'*

She peered around the corner, her eyes sweeping the dimly lit streets of a forgotten district in Ravenbrook. Beside her, Claire and Brian waited, their tensed nerves lining their foreheads. They were deep in Charles's old territory, an area once bustling with underground deals and connections, now decayed and mostly abandoned. But Nicky knew better. This place wasn't as forgotten as it seemed.

If Charles visited here often, then there must still be remnants of his network here, and if they were going to find any hard evidence of Cole's deeper involvement in Jeremy's murder, it was here, buried in the cracks of this decaying district.

"Everyone ready?" Nicky whispered, her voice low but firm.

Keisuke nodded, adjusting his earpiece. "I've got our entry point mapped. We'll need to bypass a few guards, but it's nothing we haven't handled before."

Brian crouched next to them and tightened his grip on his jacket. "I've scouted the north entrance. There's minimal activity, but we'll need to be quick. If they spot us, we won't get far."

Nicky checked her watch, counting the minutes in her head. The timing was everything, especially now. If Cole's people were already onto Gio, it would only be a matter of time before they came after her and her team, unlike what they expected. They had to move fast.

"Let's go," she said, her voice steady despite the tension. They slipped through the alleyway against the worn brick walls as they made their way toward the entrance.

As they reached the north side of the building—a crumbling warehouse that had seen better days—Keisuke pulled out his tablet, working to hack into the security system. Brian stood watch, his eyes scanning the perimeter for any sign of movement.

"Got it," Keisuke muttered after a moment, the soft click of the door unlocking echoing in the stillness. "We're in."

The door creaked open, and they slipped inside; the smell of dust, old machinery, and oil imbued the air with a certain sinister dampness. The warehouse was a maze of abandoned equipment, crates stacked haphazardly in every corner, and barrels with tar seeping out of them stocked on top of one another. But Nicky knew they weren't here for the surface-level debris. Somewhere deeper inside, hidden within the rustiness of this forgotten place, was the clue they needed—the proof that would link Cole to Jeremy's murder.

"We're looking for anything that connects Cole directly to the hit on Jeremy," Nicky whispered, her eyes sweeping the room. "Financials, correspondence, maybe even contracts."

Brian nodded, moving toward the far end of the warehouse where an old office stood. "I'll start in here. If there's anything sensitive, it'll be locked away in the back."

Nicky stayed with Claire, her eyes constantly shifting between the walls of the warehouse and the entrance they had come through. Something felt off, or maybe it was her instincts that created tension due to their last encounter at the mill. There was a stillness in the air, but not the kind that came with abandonment. It was the kind that hinted at being watched.

"We need to be fast," Nicky whispered to Claire as they moved further into the building. "Gio managed to file the lawsuit, but Cole's already making moves. We might have less time on our hands than we anticipated."

Keisuke, crouching beside Claire and Nicky, nodded, his face tight with concentration. He was already pulling up schematics of the warehouse on his tablet, looking for any hidden rooms or vaults that might contain what they needed.

As they worked, Nicky's thoughts drifted back to Gio and

the courthouse. She knew he'd faced trouble, but that was always part of the plan. Gio had his strengths in court, his ability to talk his way through impossible situations, just like he rescued her from the shackles of injustice. Nicky's strength, however, lay in the field—where things were less about words and more about instincts, timing, and action—traits she learned from being in Charles's vicinity, and she couldn't let Gio down.

The sound of a soft click brought her attention back to Claire, who had just pried open a hidden compartment in one of the iron cabinets. Inside was a stack of old files, yellowed with age but still intact.

Claire's eyes lit up. "This could be it."

They pulled the files out, spreading them across a nearby table. Nicky flipped through the pages quickly, her eyes scanning for anything that mentioned Cole, Jeremy, or the Disciples. There were references to contracts and security details, but nothing concrete yet.

Her heart sank slightly, but mustering up hope in her heart, she pushed the disappointment down. They were close. She could feel it.

Suddenly, the sound of footsteps echoed through the warehouse. Nicky froze, her hand instinctively reaching for her weapon. Claire glanced up, her eyes wide with alarm.

"Brian?" Nicky whispered into her earpiece.

"Not me," came his whispered response. "We've got

company."

Nicky swore under her breath. "How many?"

"I count two. Armed," Brian replied, peeking stealthily from the office's window.

Nicky's heart throbbed ferociously. They couldn't afford to get caught here. Not now. If Cole's people were onto them, they wouldn't hesitate to silence them—and destroy whatever evidence they had just uncovered.

"Hold your position," Nicky ordered. "Don't engage unless you have to. We need to get this evidence out of here. If they are patrolling the area, then there must be something substantial here."

"Yeah, they don't seem like they are after us. Just the regular patrolling guys," Brian concluded. "They might have seen our vehicles outside, so keep your guards up."

"Judging by their movement, they seem to be in search of something…or someone," Julian commented.

Hastily, Nicky turned to Claire, her voice low and urgent. "Pack up everything we found. We're leaving. Now."

Claire nodded, quickly gathering the files into her bag. Nicky kept her eyes on the entrance, listening to the sound of footsteps growing closer. They didn't have much time.

Brian's voice crackled in her ear again. "They're splitting up. One's heading toward your position. I'll try to divert the other."

"Be careful," Nicky whispered back.

She signaled for Claire and Keisuke to move, and together, they slipped through the shadows toward the back exit. Nicky's heartbeat drummed in her ears as she listened for the nearing footsteps, every muscle in her body coiled, ready to strike if necessary.

Just as they reached the door, the sound of a man's voice cut through the silence. "Hey! Who's there?"

Nicky cursed under her breath, pushing Claire forward. "Go! I'll cover you."

She spun around, her gun already drawn, as a figure emerged from the shadows, his weapon aimed directly at her. For a split second, time seemed to freeze.

"Drop it!" the man barked, his finger twitching over the trigger.

Sweat laced Nicky's brows while uncertainty wobbled in her eyes. Seconds felt like hours as Nicky weighed her options. She couldn't let them take her—or the files. Without hesitation, in one swift motion, she raised her gun and fired, the shot echoing through the warehouse.

The man dropped to the ground, clutching his leg as he let out a pained scream. Blood started to pool under him as he rolled on the ground.

With a hefty breath, Nicky didn't wait to see if anyone else had heard as she sprinted toward the exit—her pulse pounding in her ears. Claire and Keisuke were already outside, waiting for her with the car engine running.

"Let's go!" Claire shouted, her voice tight with fear.

Nicky dove into the passenger seat, slamming the door behind her. As they sped away from the warehouse, her breath came in ragged gasps. She glanced down at the files in Claire's bag, her heart still racing.

With all her heart, she hoped that they had what they came for. 'Or it would all have been for nothing,' Nicky thought to herself, staring at her quivering hands stained with droplets of blood.

"Brian?" Nicky called into her earpiece, her voice shaky. "You good?"

"Yeah," came his breathless reply. "Julian and I are on our way out. Meet you at the safe house."

Nicky leaned back in her seat, her mind already turning to the next step. They probably had the evidence, but they weren't out of danger yet. Cole's people were onto them now, and they wouldn't stop until the team was silenced.

"Straight to safe house?" Claire said, her eyes focused on the road.

Nicky glanced at the rearview mirror. "Yeah. But first, we need to fend off the pursuers."

As they drove deeper into the city, Nicky's thoughts drifted back to Gio, wondering if he had managed to reach the house safely or not.

The screeching sound echoed through the neighborhoods as they drifted through the streets. As Gio and Nicky stepped into the new battlefield, with every passing moment, the stakes continued to grow higher.

Chapter 17: Pieces of the Puzzle

Gio and Emily were the first to arrive back at the safehouse tucked away in the blanket of forest on the outskirts of Ravenbrook. Inside, the atmosphere was tense but somewhat warm, unlike the cold outside that clung to the windows. As they waited for Nicky and the team, Gio pored over the strategies needed to fight the next battle, distracting himself from the worrying thoughts of Nicky and her team's safety as Cole had already begun moving his pieces. Meanwhile, Emily coordinated with her contacts in the media and continued to spread rumors of General Cole and his misdeeds—tarnishing his integrity in the public and suffocating his freedom to move around brazenly.

The warmth from the fireplace flickered gently, filling the living room with a subdued light as tires screeched outside, alarming Gio as he hastily walked to the main door. Nicky and her team stood by the door, their sunken eyes and tense nerves speaking of the hurdles they had faced. Amidst the stress that lingered in between the team, Gio and Nicky's eyes locked—dispelling each worry, grief, and threat that loomed over their hearts as a warmth spread through the both of them. In each other's embrace, they found shelter from the despairs that clouded their minds.

"I was worried…I'm glad you made it back in one piece," Gio whispered as he lay his head on Nicky's shoulder.

Emily coughed, alerting Gio and Nicky as the rest of the team waited in the living room.

"Oh! We found something significant. I believe with this, we can pin Cole," said Nicky, her face reddish with embarrassment as she tucked a strand of hair behind her ear.

The team huddled together, chuckling and averting the attention from Gio and Nicky. A quiet buzz of anticipation lingered in the air between them. Outside, the world lay dormant, but inside, the weight of what they were about to face and the curiosity of how crucial the evidence that lay before them was pressed down on all of them.

Nicky leaned against the far wall, watching Gio with a soft intensity, her eyes following the way his fingers tapped rhythmically against the table as he worked through the complex structure of the case they were about to present, studying through the evidence Nicky and her team found. He looked composed, but she could see the subtle signs of strain—the way his jaw tightened, how his breath occasionally quickened. The case was filed, and now it was about preparing their best strategy.

Emily and Claire sat on the opposite side of the table, going through the files they had found, while Brian stood by the window, keeping a lookout for any intruders who might have followed them. They all knew Cole's reach could find them anywhere, but for now, they were focused. As Gio sorted through the evidence on the table, his eyes widened and confidence bolstered with each file he scanned that Nicky had procured—a cluster of damning evidence that gave him the leverage he needed in court.

"How did you guys get all this?" Gio asked, enticed by the chain of evidence he held in his hands.

"Nicky pinpointed us toward a cabin that Charles usually frequented in secret. More than his other cabins," Claire smirked, glancing at Nicky.

"But still... What were these files doing there? Did someone intentionally plant them?" Gio murmured more to himself.

"Not exactly. There was an abandoned server. With a little luck on our side, it was still functional. I used it to hack into the main server where all their data was stored. Due to the nature of their work, I assumed they must have had a separate server for the platforms they used to communicate and conduct their dealings to keep them anonymous and unique. So, every text and file they had stored in their computers or clouds were all in that linked abandoned server in the data format," Keisuke explained.

"Splendid, Keisuke. Splendid work," Gio chuckled. "That means we have access to Milton, Vince and others' files, too?"

"Unfortunately, no. The higher-ups in the organization...especially the Disciples, I believe, use a separate server for themselves, which isn't linked to the other servers. Besides, we didn't have enough time to search through everything thoroughly," Keisuke explained, adjusting his glasses.

Gio rubbed his chin, navigating his mind through the

complexities surrounding the Disciples. The faint sound of a news broadcast filtered in from a TV screen tucked into the corner of the room, grasping everyone's attention. Emily had already ensured that the media storm was well underway as her face lit up upon seeing the screen.

"Breaking news tonight: A high-profile lawsuit has been filed against General Cole, a decorated military officer who, according to sources, is tied to a series of illegal activities, including the murder of whistleblower Jeremy Denver. Cole, once hailed as a patriot, is now facing allegations of corruption, cover-ups, and direct involvement in assassination plots. Whistleblowers and insiders claim that Cole used his position of power to protect the criminal dealings of Milton's organization, shielding them from the law and orchestrating a campaign to eliminate those who got too close to the truth. The case could unravel years of corruption at the highest levels of the military..."

Gio's lips pressed into a thin line as the broadcast continued, his mind already racing through how the chaos caused by the media would influence the upcoming trial. It was risky. Public opinion could sway jurors, but it could also create backlash if they weren't careful. Emily was a genius at using the press, but now it was up to him to use that momentum in court.

"Good job, Em. This will certainly help," said Gio as he straightened, a slight groan escaping his lips as he stretched his back, but his eyes remained sharp. "Alright," Gio began, his voice calm and deliberate. "Let's break this down methodically."

He picked up a marker from the table and moved to the whiteboard against the wall. "First, we start with the financials. These records of off-the-books payments made to someone within his network are essential—my guess? It's the hitman, and we'll play it that way. We know Cole used his military accounts to disguise the payments as security expenses. They'll try to argue it was for official purposes, so we have to show how the timing of these payments—made right before Jeremy's death—cannot be a coincidence."

Gio drew two lines on the board, connecting Cole's offshore accounts to the payments made to the hitman.

"We don't need to prove that Cole directly pulled the trigger. What we need is to demonstrate that he facilitated and orchestrated the hit. That's the first key point: means. The financials show that Cole had the ability to make it happen."

Emily stepped forward, glancing at the board. "But how do we make sure the jury sees that? Couldn't Cole's lawyers argue that these payments were routine, that they were meant for any number of military operations?"

Gio gave her a small, appreciative smile. "Good question. That's where the security clearance comes in. We introduce the clearance documents right after the financials, showing that Cole gave the hitman access to restricted military zones. These clearances are not standard procedure, especially for someone not actively involved in military operations. We hammer home that this was highly unusual."

He added a third line to the board, connecting the payments to the clearance requests. "What this does is establish not just the means but also the method—potential MO. Cole didn't just authorize payments—he made sure the people who could execute the hit had everything they needed to carry it out."

Claire interjected, "What about the correspondence between Cole and Milton? That's still vague, and the defense could argue that *'tying up loose ends'* could mean anything. We only have the text sent by Cole to the anonymous, and the receiver's identity is literally untraceable."

"True," Gio acknowledged, "but vagueness works both ways. For now, our focus should be on Cole. We use the correspondence as circumstantial evidence. The vaguer it is, the easier it is for us to suggest what they were really discussing. Cole's lawyers will argue that it's open to interpretation, but we don't need to prove beyond all doubt—just beyond reasonable doubt. The correspondence shows intent. It shows Cole was directly involved with some malicious organization and aware of Jeremy's whistleblowing activities."

He turned to the group, his voice taking on a more intense tone. "The key is how we present it. The timeline is everything. We need the jury to see this case as a step-by-step progression—one where every action Cole took led directly to Jeremy's death. First, he funded the operation.

Then, he authorized the access. Finally, he communicated with the one in command—assuming it's Milton as far as we know—to ensure the job got done. Each piece of evidence builds on the last, and by the time we're done, the jury won't be able to see any other conclusion."

There was a brief silence as the team absorbed the strategy and the analytical precision with which Gio dissected the case. Nicky couldn't help but admire how his mind worked, his ability to work through a clutter of evidence and simplify it into a clear, irrefutable narrative.

"Once we've laid all that out," Gio continued, "we introduce Jeremy's whistleblower reports. We show that Jeremy was about to expose Cole's illegal activities, which establishes a motive. Cole knew Jeremy was getting too close, so he took steps to ensure he was eliminated. The false reports labeling Jeremy as a security threat will be key in proving that Cole was setting up the justification for the hit."

Gio's gaze swept the room, his eyes narrowing in concentration. "This is the pincer. Means, method, and motive. We corner Cole on all sides. By the time we're finished, he won't be able to argue that this was anything but premeditated murder."

Nicky, who had been quietly watching, finally spoke up. "And if the defense tries to poke holes in the financials or the security clearance? What if they manage to discredit one part of our case?"

"That's where Emily's media coverage comes in," Gio

said, glancing over at Emily. "We're not just fighting this battle in court. The media is already turning public opinion against Cole. By the time we go to trial, the jury will already have an idea of who Cole is—corrupt, dangerous, and willing to do anything to protect himself. If the defense tries to poke holes, we push harder with the emotional narrative: Jeremy was a hero trying to expose corruption, and Cole killed him for it. People care about stories, not just facts."

The news broadcast in the background continued, the voice of the anchor sounding almost triumphant.

"In related news, several reports are pouring in from anonymous sources, claiming they were silenced by General Cole's network of power and influence. While their identities remain protected, these individuals have corroborated claims that Cole orchestrated a series of illegal activities ranging from financial embezzlement to murder."

Emily's eyes flicked toward the screen. "The more stories like that, the harder it'll be for the defense to gain any traction. The jury will already have a narrative in their heads."

Gio nodded. "Exactly. Public perception will be our shield in case anything goes wrong. But our case is strong. We've built it piece by piece, and now it's about execution. We go in methodically, follow the timeline, and leave no room for Cole's lawyers to wiggle out."

There was a quiet hum of approval from the group, the tension easing slightly as they felt the strength of their case take shape. Nicky stood close to Gio, her hand brushing lightly against his arm as she leaned in.

"You've really thought of everything," she said softly, her voice carrying a mix of admiration and affection.

Gio's eyes softened as he looked at her. "I've had a lot of help," he murmured, his hand resting gently over hers. The warmth between them was palpable, a quiet moment of intimacy amidst the chaos of their situation.

Nicky smiled, her fingers curling around his. "We're going to bring him down. I know we are."

Before Gio could respond, his phone buzzed on the table. He glanced at the screen, his brow furrowing slightly. "It's the DA's office."

He tapped the screen and read the message, his face shifting from concentration to a calm resolve. "The trial date's been set."

Nicky's hand tightened around his. "When?"

Gio looked up, meeting her gaze. "Two weeks. We've got two weeks to finish gathering everything and prepare."

For the first time in weeks, Gio felt a flicker of hope. After a long and tiring fight on the streets, the battle of his abilities was finally here. The plague of corruption, murder, and betrayal that had enveloped them for so long was starting to dissipate, and at the center of it all, he had found something more than just a case worth fighting for—his deepening love for Nicky.

She looked up at him, her eyes reflecting the flicker of the firelight, and for a moment, everything else faded. The trial, the danger, the sleepless nights—they all seemed distant. What mattered now was this moment between them, the quiet understanding that they had been through hell together and come out stronger.

"I don't know what I'd have done without you," Nicky admitted, her voice low—vulnerability imbued in her words. "All of this is only happening because you kept pushing, kept going when I wasn't sure I could."

Gio tilted his head, a small smile curving his lips. "You're giving me too much credit, Nicky. I wouldn't be here without you either."

Nicky shook her head, stepping closer, her hand reaching to cup his face, her thumb brushing gently across his cheek. "No, Gio. You've been the strongest one here. You've always known what to do, even when I didn't. And... I've come to realize I don't just need you in this fight. I need you."

Gio's breath hitched slightly, his heart pounding against his chest as his eyes immersed in her affectionate gaze, seeing the depth of her words. For Nicky, his gaze felt like a sanctuary—in its shade, she felt whole. Gio, who always seemed so steady and composed, was letting her see just how much she meant to him. And in that moment, the walls that she had built around herself started to crumble.

Without another word, she leaned in, pressing her lips to

his in a kiss that was tender but filled with the weight of everything unsaid between them. The tension, the fear, the uncertainty—it all melted away as they held each other, the connection between them growing stronger with every heartbeat.

"You know," she said quietly, her voice low, "I've been running so long I almost forgot what it feels like to stop. But with you... I feel like I finally found something worth fighting for."

Gio's breath caught in his throat as he looked down at her, the intensity of her words hitting him harder than any legal battle. He lifted a hand, brushing a strand of hair behind her ear, his touch lingering. "You're not running anymore, Nicky. Not with me."

She smiled a soft, genuine smile that made his chest tighten. Time slowed around them as they held onto each other, the fire crackling softly in the background. Gio's hand still rested on her waist as they prepared to face what lay ahead. His faith in the resolve—protecting Nicky—solidified. Gazing deep into her eyes, Gio assured himself, *'The battle had only just begun, but now, I had everything I needed to bring Cole down. And together, we would win.'*

Chapter 18: A Trial of Nerves

Each day of the two weeks leading up to the trial was laced with tension and pressure of preparations for Gio and the team. Feverishly, everyone grouped together to scour through piles of evidence in an orderly manner as Gio instructed, revisited the list of potential witnesses Cole's attorneys could bring up and drafted their own witnesses. They sharpened their strategy with meticulous precision, like surgeons preparing for a high-risk operation.

The weight of the case hunched Gio's shoulders as this was the first blow they would deal against the evil they were against—he knew he had to make it count. Nights turned into days as Gio pushed against time, defiling the natural order of working and pouring his utmost into scrutinizing the case he was about to present.

Even as the team operated in high gear, Gio found it impossible to ignore the gnawing presence of the silence of Cole that had been creeping into his life. Every day, his mind throbbed with the feeling that threats would start pouring in, but nothing came aside from the haunting silence—the silence that plunged him deeper into the doubts. *'What were they planning? Do they have some hidden card up their sleeve? This silence is unusual.'* Such thoughts continued to spiral around his head. As the trial neared, the eerie feeling in Gio's mind grew in intensity, almost as if Cole and his camp had found a way to discard his case. Gio tried to shake it off, focusing on the work that lay ahead, but the thoughts stayed with him, echoing in the back of his mind.

The day before the trial, Gio received a particularly chilling voicemail from an unknown number—a raspy voice saying, "You pride yourself on being a lawyer, I suppose. That courtroom shall be your grave."

A quivering sensation crawled down Gio's spine as he played the message over and over again, trying to discern any clues in the voice, but there was nothing identifiable—the masked man who had followed Gio since he took on this case, it wasn't him. The doubts that clouded his mind intensified like a thick fog around his brain—a sickening feeling plagued his morale as his instincts told him the fight in the courtroom would be brutal.

"What's wrong?" Nicky asked as she noticed Gio's shaken eyes.

"Nothing... I just don't know what they have got up their sleeve," Gio muttered, poring over the scattered documents on his desk.

"I have seen you in the courtroom, Gio. No one can beat you in there," Nicky reassured.

"Let's see," Gio said in a low voice, his eyes lingering over the name of the attorney Cole had chosen—Valerie Chambers, a seasoned attorney with a reputation for dismantling her opposition with surgical precision.

Sighing out the worries, Gio assured himself the evidence they had gathered was concrete and couldn't be discredited no matter who he was up against. He wore the mask of confidence and averted his focus on the job—his resolve hardening, fueled by the weight of justice, as he steeled himself for the battle ahead.

Finally, the day of the trial arrived—anticipation pinched each of their hearts as the team followed Gio into the court. The atmosphere in the courtroom was imbued with a different energy that morning—alive, electric tension humming through its hallways. Eyes of strangers lingered over them as though everyone had gathered there, knowing well this trial was no ordinary one. Spectators filled the galley—reporters, curious onlookers, and others who had heard the buzz surrounding the case. Cole was a man with connections, and his notoriety added an air of spectacle to the proceedings.

Gio entered the courtroom dressed in a neatly stitched jet-black suit paired with an off-white shirt, his every step measured, his face a picture of calm—his mere appearance entranced the courtroom with his charms.

Despite the storm of the last two weeks, he appeared as sharp as ever in his tailored navy suit, his briefcase swinging effortlessly at his side. The room quieted as he took his place at the prosecution table, his team arranged neatly beside him, ready for battle. Across the room sat Cole, flanked by his formidable defense team led by Valerie Chambers. She sat calmly, flipping through her notes, her icy demeanor a stark contrast to the fire Gio's team was about to bring.

Cole himself sat with an air of smugness that made Gio's blood boil. He exuded a sort of invincibility as though the courtroom were merely a formality—just another inconvenience in his life. His tailored gray suit was immaculate, his hair slicked back, and a half-smile curled on his lips, suggesting he believed, deep down, that the outcome of this trial had already been decided in his favor. Gio locked eyes with him for a brief moment before turning his attention back to his team. Today wasn't about theatrics. It wasn't about the bravado that Cole seemed to thrive on. Today was about setting the stage for justice—a stage Gio had meticulously prepared for over the past two weeks—since the time this fight against the Disciples started.

When the judge called the trial to order and directed the jury's attention to Gio for his opening statement, the room seemed to hold its breath. Gio stood, his posture confident but not rigid, and approached the jury with disarming ease as if he were simply having a conversation with a group of close friends.

"Ladies and gentlemen of the jury," he began, his voice warm and rich, immediately pulling the twelve individuals in front of him into his orbit. "We're here today because the truth matters. It's as simple as that. The truth matters. What you're going to hear over the next days— maybe weeks—is a story that reveals the actions of a man who thought he could bend the truth, manipulate it, twist it to serve his own interests, without ever facing the consequences—a man gone senile with the power he held in his hands. The very power that was bestowed on him by you—by us hardworking people of this town. But the truth has a way of surfacing. And when it does, it shines a light so bright that not even the most skillful of manipulators can hide from it."

He paused, letting the gravity of his words settle in, allowing the jury to absorb the meaning behind them. His pacing was deliberate but not slow, his hands gesturing lightly as though he were painting a picture in the air.

"This case is about Cole," he continued, turning slightly to glance at the defendant, who sat stoic, his eyes narrowing slightly. "It's about the decisions he made. It's about the choices that led to the crime you're going to hear about—the lies, the deceit, the manipulation. And over the course of this trial, my team and I are going to show you, beyond a streak of a doubt, that Cole is guilty of the crimes he stands accused of."

Gio's eyes ricocheted from the first to the last member of the jury, reading their expressions, ensuring that he had their undivided attention. "This case is not about proving guilt. It's about justice. We gather here today to make sure that when someone like Cole betrays trust, manipulates the system, and breaks the law, they are held accountable. People like him bleed us dry and leave us to rot in their filth while they relish the luxuries they have by robbing us. There are many others like him still lavishly sitting in their mansions, joking about our struggles and planning how they would rip us off next. We are going to prove that Cole is guilty—not by assumption, not by hearsay, but by irrefutable facts."

Letting the weight of the moment hang in the air, Gio took a breath before continuing, "By the end of this trial, you'll see his fingerprints all over this crime. I'm sure, considering how charming my colleague Valerie can be in twisting the details, you'll be told many stories to distract you from the truth. The bare truth that we will unveil before you through evidence that cannot be ignored."

With his opening statement infused in the jury's minds, his words instilling a sense of patriotism for justice in their hearts, Gio thanked the jury and returned to his seat.

Valerie Chambers stood next, a slow, calculated smile curling her lips as she approached the jury. She wasted no time attempting to match Gio's warmth. Instead, she relied on her sharp intellect and her unfazed demeanor, which gave the impression that she was above the theatrics of the courtroom.

"Ladies and gentlemen," she began, her voice smooth but with a pointed edge, "what you just heard was a very compelling story. I'll give Mr. Gio credit—he knows how to weave a narrative that tugs at the heartstrings and paints a picture of guilt before you've even heard a single fact. But this courtroom isn't a theater. It's not a place for stories or fiction. It's a place for facts. And the fact is, my client, Cole, is not guilty of the crimes he's been accused of."

She paused for effect, her eyes narrowing slightly as she

shifted her stance. "What we're going to show you is not a tale of manipulation and deceit, but a series of unfortunate circumstances—coincidences, even—that have been twisted by the prosecution to fit their narrative. They want you to believe that everything you hear is tied up neatly in a bow, pointing directly to my client. But as the facts unfold, you'll see that the picture is far more complicated than they would have you believe."

Chambers' voice was measured, never rising, never falling too far from her calculated cadence. She was clearly trying to set the jury's expectations and position Gio's argument as one driven by emotion rather than fact.

"My client has been caught in the crosshairs of a situation beyond his control," she continued. "And while the prosecution would have you believe that he orchestrated this grand scheme, the reality is much simpler. Cole is innocent, and by the end of this trial, you'll see that the prosecution's case is built on nothing but sand."

Chambers concluded with a soft, confident smile and returned to her seat. The atmosphere in the room shifted yet again as the battle lines had officially been drawn.

With the opening statements behind them, the first day of trial began in earnest. He stood calmly at his desk, smoothing out his tie as the judge signaled for the proceedings to begin. As per the plan, Gio was to present a key piece of evidence that would cement the narrative he had built.

The courtroom was still as if it, too, could sense the

gravity of what was to come. Gio approached the podium, eyes scanning the jury with confidence. He turned slightly, addressing both the judge and the jury with his next words.

"Your Honor, I would like to present Exhibit B—a piece of evidence that I believe will make things very clear for everyone in this courtroom."

He motioned to Keisuke, who stepped forward with a sleek black tablet. The lights dimmed as the courtroom's screen flickered to life, displaying a series of images and documents. The silence was deafening as everyone's eyes peeled towards the screen.

"This," Gio began, walking towards the screen with a pointer, "is a ledger. But not just any ledger—this is a digital record of Cole's finances over a three-year period, hidden within encrypted servers we recently gained access to. What you see here are payments made to various individuals under shell companies, but notice the consistency in the amounts and dates."

He zoomed in on the screen, highlighting a set of recurring payments to an offshore account under a seemingly innocuous company name, but the amounts—large sums wired consistently on the same dates each month—hinted at something more.

"These aren't just business payments. They were made to the very individuals Mr. Cole claims to have no association with—the people implicated in the cover-up of illegal activities, as he has proclaimed to be not guilty."

He paused, walking toward the jury with measured steps. His eyes found the foreman's, and he held the gaze just long enough to deepen the impact of his next statement. But Chambers wasn't going to let him solidify his opinion in the jury's mind—she was quick to object and raise questions about the authenticity of the evidence.

"Objection, Your Honor! The evidence presented by Mr. Rossi is, for all we know, fabricated evidence. No report here suggests that the evidence was obtained legally and is, in fact, related to my client," she said, waving the copy of the evidence in her hand.

"Miss Valerie, I admire your enthusiasm, but all the evidence has been cleared through forensics and is deemed legitimate. If there are still doubts about the evidence, Your Honor, I'll call in the forensics team as witnesses."

Judge Westwood glanced from Valerie to Gio, weighing the arguments before giving her ruling. "Overruled. The evidence will be admitted, but Ms. Chambers, you will have ample opportunity to cross-examine the experts when the time comes."

"What we have here is not a simple pattern of usual transactions. It's proof—a direct link between Cole and the criminal enterprises he has funded. This is the key, ladies and gentlemen. The key that shows how he funneled money to silence those who could expose him and to finance those who carried out his dirty work."

Gio nodded graciously and continued. He resumed

pointing to the screen, where a list of transactions blinked in bold.

"As I was saying, these payments—"

"Objection!" Valerie interrupted again, her voice rising slightly, now with a tone of incredulity. "Counsel is implying illegal conduct without direct evidence of wrongdoing."

This time, Gio didn't turn away from the screen. He responded swiftly, his voice calm but firm. "Your Honor, I am merely presenting the facts as they appear in the records. The jury will make its own conclusions."

Judge Westwood, clearly growing impatient with the interruptions, leaned forward slightly. "Ms. Chambers sustained in part. Mr. Gio, do refrain from implying guilt at this stage. Stick to the facts, please."

With that, Gio gave a small nod, a flicker of satisfaction in his expression. He knew the damage had already been done—he'd gotten the jury's attention. They were already beginning to connect the dots in their minds.

Returning to his focus on the transactions, Gio pushed forward, undeterred by the back-and-forth objections. "Ladies and gentlemen, let's take a look at the next series of payments. These transfers were all made to the same account, under different names, but the routing details show they were funneled through identical offshore banks."

Valerie shifted in her seat, clearly preparing for another

round, but Gio anticipated it. Before she could raise her hand again, he swiftly pointed to a highlighted transaction. "Objection, Ms. Chambers?"

Valerie narrowed her eyes but held her ground. "Not yet, counsel," she said coldly, but the tension in her voice betrayed her frustration.

Satisfied, Gio moved on, presenting another chart showing the flow of money across multiple shell companies. As he delved into the timeline, showing how the transfers lined up perfectly with key events in the criminal conspiracy, Valerie could no longer remain silent.

"Objection, Your Honor!" she practically shouted, rising from her seat this time. "Counsel is speculating about intent! These transactions alone do not prove any form of conspiracy!"

The judge's eyes flicked to Gio, waiting for his response.

"Your Honor," Gio began calmly, "I am merely laying the groundwork for the jury to see the full picture. The experts will explain the mechanics of these transactions in detail. We are not speculating—we are showing facts, numbers, and connections."

The judge nodded—her tone firm but fair. "Overruled, but Mr. Gio, you are treading close to conjecture. Keep it factual."

Gio smiled slightly, then turned back to the jury. He knew when to pull back, and now was the time to refocus on the hard evidence.

"Let's look at the next document," Gio said, motioning toward the screen, "an email conversation between Mr. Cole and one of his associates. Here, you'll see a direct order for funds to be transferred to an unmarked account—along with an instruction to 'keep this quiet.'"

He turned the jury's attention to the damning words on the screen, highlighted in yellow for emphasis. The words spoke for themselves, and this time, Valerie didn't object. There was no objection that could erase what was clearly in front of them.

Gio glanced at the judge. "Your Honor, I move to admit these emails as evidence."

"Objection!" Valerie rose again, her voice tight with controlled anger, but this time, she kept her emotions composed. "Emails like these could easily be taken out of context. We have no way of verifying who wrote them or whether they are related to the financial transactions in question. This is circumstantial, at best."

Gio, ready for this challenge, faced the judge once more. "Your Honor, these emails were obtained directly from the defendant's source, and we will present witnesses who can verify the chain of custody. Furthermore, forensic analysis has confirmed that these communications originated from Mr. Cole's private email server."

Judge Westwood considered the argument carefully, her fingers tapping lightly on her desk. "Overruled. The emails will be admitted. Ms. Chambers, you'll have your opportunity to question their relevance later."

Valerie clenched her jaw, clearly displeased with the judge's decision, but forced to sit back down.

Gio took the opportunity to drive his point home. "Ladies and gentlemen, these documents paint a very clear picture. There is a trail—a well-concealed, deliberately hidden trail—that ties Mr. Cole directly to these illegal activities."

The room was so quiet you could hear the shifting of seats as the jury leaned in. Gio knew he had them. This time, he didn't need his charms to sway the jury's opinion, but the truth—people needed to understand and decide that the truth prevails.

For a moment, the only sound was the soft buzzing of the projector. The jurors exchanged glances, their attention now completely locked on Gio. He had them right where he wanted them.

He turned his focus back to the bench. "I have no further evidence to present at this time, Your Honor."

The judge nodded. "Very well. We'll reconvene tomorrow for further arguments."

The gavel came down with a sharp crack, but the tension in the room remained. As Gio returned to his seat, he could feel the eyes of the jurors on him, their minds working through the tip of the evidence he had just dropped in their laps. He gave a slight smile—knowing that the first blow was a success, but the triumph was still far from their grasp. The battle had just begun, and he knew that Valerie Chambers wasn't done yet. Today, he might have subdued her, but considering her tactics, she'll strike back harder.

Valerie rose from her seat, her face composed but her eyes sharp. She leaned slightly toward Gio as she passed his table. "This isn't over, Gio. You may have gotten through today, but tomorrow..."

Gio didn't look up, but he responded, his voice firm and calm. "I'll be ready, Valerie. Always am."

With that, she walked out of the courtroom, her heels clicking on the marble floors, already strategizing her next move. Gio remained seated for a moment longer, glancing down at the files on his table. There was still much to do, but for today, he had laid the foundation. The real fight, however, was far from over—and he still didn't know what Valerie had up her sleeve, for her today's impatience was deliberate to throw us off. However, the seed of doubt had been planted as he noticed some people in the jury glancing at Cole already as if he were guilty.

The judge's gavel struck, signaling the end of the day's session, but the tension in the room throbbed relentlessly. Gio slumped his face in his palms, running a hand through his hair as he took a breath. Day one had gone according to plan.

Tomorrow, they would see what Valerie has up her arsenal. Emily approached from behind, tapping Gio on the shoulder.

"Do you guys have some history? You and Valerie," she asked.

"Rivalry, you can say. A long one, but we don't have time for that. Tomorrow will be rough, so we need to prepare ourselves as much as we can," Gio said as he walked out of the courtroom with the same confidence he walked into it.

Chapter 19: The Veiled Truth

The air in Gio's office was thick with tension—his thoughts pored over what Valerie had up her sleeve while Nicky and the rest of the team scavenged through Charles's and his disciples' hideouts, searching for any piece of clue. The day continued to trickle away with stress nagging at Gio's mind—his motives weren't just to put Cole behind bars, but to put the whole murder mystery revolving around Charles to rest in this ongoing trial—hit Vince and others while they watch the show of their own man's demise.

Soon, the night veiled the skies, and Gio's phone rang, breaking him out of his trance.

"Gio...don't show up for the trial tomorrow," Nicky's hefty voice echoed from the other side of the phone.

"What do you mean? What's going on, Nicky?" Gio inquired, jumping out of his seat.

"I think we are on the cusp of something. If you don't go, the trial will be delayed, and I think... I think we found something that would need time to be studied," Nicky explained in a hurry.

"I don't understand, Nicky. What did you guys find?" Gio asked frantically, his mind throbbing with worry yet anticipation.

"We are short on time. I'll tell you when we get back; we are on our way right now," she rambled and cut the call.

Each second of wait weighed heavy on Gio's shoulders as his eyes sank even more with each hour passing. *'What could they have uncovered? Were they being chased? What's going on?'* Such thoughts ran courses through his mind until finally, the whole squad arrived after midnight—their faces a mix of fear and excitement.

"Thank God," Gio murmured. "What happened out there?"

"We were scouring through the cabins the disciples once used...some were guarded, some unguarded...but we found this," Claire explained as she handed an aged journal to Gio.

"What's this?" Gio asked, inspecting the rustic pages.

"Wagner's journal," Nicky answered, her voice stern and confident.

Hastily, Gio marched to his office and started reading through the journal—it had everything transcribed in it since the day Wagner joined Charles's organization. As he read through the entries, Gio's mind throbbed with the countless questions running through his head, but one doubt...one suspicion lingered at the front of his mind, *'Was Wagner the man who kept following us? Threatening us?'*

The deeper he dug into it, the more Gio's thoughts turned back to one name: Wagner.

Nicky stood by the window, her arms crossed, studying the street below. She had been quiet ever since Gio started studying through the journal. It hadn't revealed everything, but it had left breadcrumbs—Cryptic symbols, strange markings. It was all there, yet incomplete.

"Why did Wagner record all this?" Gio asked aloud.

"I think the question should be…why was Wagner at Charles's mansion the night he was killed?" Nicky asked, breaking her silence.

Gio flipped the pages and studied the marking engraved on the front page of the journal—the same symbol that was carved on Charles's bedroom floor.

"I think there's more to it here… Wagner was close to Charles, but he's been hiding something. The blood on the drapes, the carvings—he's involved, but not in the way we thought," Gio voiced his thoughts.

"Are you sure we are not overlooking the killer?" Nicky retorted.

"It's just my hunch. Something's fishy. Why would Wagner leave something of such importance just like that? No. He's been calculated all along. Come to think of it…if he's the one who's been stalking us… He threatened us but didn't kill us even when he had the chance," Gio murmured, his eyes narrowing with each word.

"There's not much time to waste. I trust your instincts, and we should talk to him to get more answers out of him," Nicky added as she pulled her cashmere coat from the chair.

"You are right. Our answers lie with him. Cole can wait a day," said Gio as he followed Nicky out of the house.

They drove through the night, making their way to Wagner's mansion. Mustering up every bit of courage and quelling every question in his mind, Gio knocked, but there was no answer.

Just as he was about to knock for the third time, a text popped up on his phone: *"Come to the café to the north on the outskirts of the town."*

"It's him," Gio whispered and hurried back to the car.

"How did he know?" Nicky asked, sitting shotgun.

"Just like he did every time before," Gio sighed.

The café was quiet, a small, nondescript place on the outskirts of Ravenbrook. Wagner was already there to meet Gio, but both knew the meeting was more than casual. It was an interrogation disguised as a simple conversation—a meeting of revelations.

Wagner sat at the table by the window, waiting. He had already set the stage. Nicky was nearby, keeping watch. This was their chance to get to the heart of the mystery—to uncover what Wagner had been hiding. The door chimed softly as Gio entered, his expression calm but guarded. He moved toward the table with an air of quiet confidence, and Wagner rose to greet him, shaking his hand. However, the tension between them was palpable—all the unanswered questions making the air quiver between them.

"It's good to meet you, Wagner," Gio greeted.

Wagner smiled, but his eyes remained hollow of

emotions, "Your gaze is different from what it was back in the mill, Gio. You have been looking for answers, and the time has come for you to know."

Despite his doubts being answered—that Wagner was the one who kept threatening—Gio remained calm; this wasn't the answer he needed anymore—the question was, *'Why?'*

They sat, and for a moment, there was silence. Gio watched Wagner closely, every movement, every glance.

"Why did you leave it in that hideout?" Gio asked as he pulled out Wagner's journal.

Staring blankly with almost amused eyes at the journal, Wagner met Gio's inquiring gaze, "Would we be here if you hadn't found it, Mr. Rossi?"

"Why?" Gio muttered.

"There's much to uncover and no time, Mr. Rossi. Ask the right questions, and we'll get where we both want to go faster," Wagner answered, sipping through his coffee.

"Why were you in Charles's room the night of his murder?" Gio asked.

"So you saw the symbol… I was too late. It wasn't the night of the murder, Mr. Rossi, you are talking about. Although I was there that night, too, I couldn't save him in time. But then you took on his case. I saw your determination, so I carved the symbol in hopes of this day to come."

"But you threatened me every time I got near to some

clue, Wagner. That isn't helping," Gio retorted, keeping his composure as everything scattered in his mind.

"I had to, Mr. Rossi. I couldn't let you get too close, or it would have been my neck on the line. Nor could I let you stray far from the objective. I had to be cautious as to how I would play this. For the sake of both of us," Wagner replied sternly. "Sorry for that punch, by the way."

"I-It's fine. But you still haven't answered why you did all this. The coded messages. The symbols. The blood on drapes... Was that your doing too?"

"I'll answer, Mr. Rossi. You see, even though I was Charles's disciple, we had a complicated relationship, but I never hated him. I looked up to that man. He had certain beliefs and rituals—things not everyone could understand, but I was loyal, for he had taught me ways of life. I rushed to his mansion as soon as I discovered that they were going to murder him in cold blood, but I couldn't in time. So, I went undercover...assumed the role of keeping you at a distance without getting you killed so you could bring the murderers to light," Wagner explained.

Gio's pulse quickened with each detail—and in some part of his soul, he felt sympathy for the man whom he despised wholeheartedly once. "So, you know who murdered Charles?"

Nerves tightened around Charles's forehead, his fingers quivering with anger as he clutched his coffee mug.

"Agnes," he whispered.

"Wait...Agnes McAllister? This makes no sense," Gio jumped from his seat. "She helped Nicky. I understand she had some history with Milton, but... No. Why should I believe you?"

"It was all a farce to throw you off track while she covered her tracks. Agnes conspired with Milton and Vince—and gave them positions of power. You must be thinking about what she gained out of it: wealth and power. With this, Milton and Vince had become pawns of her while she shuffled the pieces from behind the scenes. She had proof of how they orchestrated the murder, but Milton and Vince were too blind to harness a fraction of Charles's wealth that they overlooked the big picture," Wagner explained thoroughly—his fingernails plunged deeper into his palm. "I knew you wouldn't be able to apprehend the real culprit, so I decided to help you. As for the proof you seek, it's buried under the same floor where we fought, Mr. Rossi. A stairway shrouded under old machinery leads to the basement, where you can find traces of their planning, their collaboration in Charles's murder."

"This is... I... It's horrible," Gio mumbled, rubbing his forehead. "Why didn't you come forward before?"

"I had to be cautious, Mr. Rossi. I needed to know that you would take action if provided the right opportunity and arsenal. By going up against Cole, you proved yourself; hence, you gained my trust," Wagner smirked, raising his cup of coffee as a gesture of commendation.

With the scrambled pieces of the puzzle littering his mind, Gio ventured out of the café and joined Nicky in the car. Making sense of the haze of thoughts that clouded his mind, he explained every bit of detail to her—with each detail, her face got painted with the same confusion that tainted Gio's face.

As the morning sun soared in the sky, shedding its first light across the town, Gio and Nicky made their way to the old mill—in a hurry to tear past the fabric of truth and lies—to the heart of reality. On their way, they called Emily and the others to the old mill.

The old mill loomed ahead of them, its dark silhouette casting eerie shadows in the morning light. Gio, Nicky, and Emily approached the building, their footsteps echoing in the stillness while Claire and others kept watch around the mill.

"This place is as creepy as it was before," Nicky muttered as they entered the mill. "How could we miss this secret basement?"

"It's well hidden, but thank Wagner for that," Gio replied. "We are looking for an old machine wrapped under the dusty maroon cloth."

After gazing around for a while, they found a small machine catching rust under a maroon rag. Pulling the rag off, Gio proceeded as Wagner had instructed him—pull the lever of the machine; it will open the path to the basement, he had said. Following the manual provided by Wagner, Gio pulled the lever, and a loud creaking sound echoed through the mill.

Gasping amidst a cloud of dust, the trio met each other's gaze and strolled onto the stairs leading to the basement. The stairs creaked under their weight, and soon, they stood in a narrow hallway, the air thick with dust. Gio's heart pounded as they entered a large room, its walls lined with old, decaying furniture. But it was the table in the center that drew their attention—a weathered, wooden structure covered in papers.

"Search for anything that seems valuable to our case," Gio instructed, and the trio dispersed in the dusty room, searching each nook and cranny of the room.

"Does this lamp count, too?" Emily chuckled, holding a small, tea-cup-shaped lamp.

"No," Gio replied sternly, unamused. "Focus, Emily. And don't leave any trace that could tell them someone was here."

"Roger that," Emily replied and marched back to the cabinets stacked with old files and ledgers.

After scouring through the room for a while, Emily's voice tore through the silence between them.

"Hey, guys. I think I found something," she mumbled.

Hurriedly, Gio and Nicky rushed to her, staring at the old ledger she held in her hands.

"What is it?" Nicky asked.

"Details of Charles's murder...and there was this map tucked in between it—layout of Charles's mansion and details of when it was vulnerable and when not," Emily replied with a shaky voice.

"So, Wagner was right...but this doesn't prove it was Agnes or any other person," Gio conjectured while he inspected the clues they had found. "Wait...open the last page, Emily," Gio said in a hurry as he saw a glimpse of something while Emily was flipping through the ledger.

A sketch of a person fitting the description that Agnes had described to Gio in their conversation when he followed up, asking if she had seen the murderer. The same dress, disguise hat, gender, and height of the person—each detail was specified on the side.

"She told me the exact description when I asked her about the murderer... This is... She planned her response and consulted with Vince and Milton before I had even begun my investigation," Gio murmured, more to himself as his eyes trembled in disbelief.

For some reason, a tinge of fear mixed with admiration lingered through his soul as he stared at the sketch.

'This is genius...horrendously genius,' he thought to himself. Within the ledger are the plans for how Vince would take over the organization after Charles's demise, while Milton would act like the leader for appearances. Each detail was written as to how things would be executed after Charles's murder.

"I think we have it…We can finally get them, Nicky," Gio's voice trembled with excitement.

With tears in her eyes, Nicky pulled Gio in a hug—her heart whispering words of gratitude as relief washed over her.

"Wait, how would we prove Agnes's role in this?" Emily chimed in.

"I have a plan for that. Tomorrow, we bring them all down. The very plan they thought they orchestrated by framing Cole, we would make it a noose around their necks," said Gio, his words thrumming with courage and resilience—a resolve with which he started this hunt for justice.

With evidence in his hands and plans of cornering Agnes McAllister, Gio drove away under the crimson shade of the sinking sun. The hope for justice only seemed a few steps away now, and he was ready to walk through it and liberate Nicky from the shadow of injustice.

Chapter 20: The Final Judgment

The courtroom buzzed with an electric tension as Gio and his team marched in—their resolve bolstered by the strategy they curated last night to pin Agnes and others. Each one of them knew this was no longer just the trial of General Cole; it had become a sweeping indictment of the influential figures who lurked in the shadows, puppeteering chaos from behind the masks of responsible citizens—Agnes McAllister, Milton, and Vince.

Gio's confidence was as sharp as the freshly ironed lapels of his suit, and his objective was clear: bring to light the roles of Agnes, Milton, and Vince, unraveling the conspiracy that had taken lives and disrupted countless others.

As the jury took their seats, a hush fell over the courtroom. The press had filled the back rows, notebooks and recorders at the ready, cameras capturing every tense moment.

Gio gathered his files, his mind sharp, his objective clear: to dismantle the defenses of these powerful people in full view of the court, forcing them to face justice for Charles Blackwood's murder and the conspiracy they had spun to frame Nicky. He scanned the jury, observing the mixture of anticipation and doubt that hung in the air. Averting his gaze, he saw Agnes and the disciples sitting in the court; pride washed over their faces.

Gio stood, his voice steady as he addressed the

courtroom. "Ladies and gentlemen of the jury, over the past few days, you have been shown evidence of General Cole's role in these events. But what has emerged from this investigation is far bigger. It's a coordinated plot—a conspiracy involving influential figures who, out of greed and ambition, took Charles Blackwood's life. Today, we will not only expose Cole's involvement but also the direct actions of Agnes McAllister, Milton, and Vince in orchestrating his murder."

The silence in the courtroom was unnerving. Shocked murmurs rippled through the crowd as Agnes's face paled. Milton's face twitched as Vince immediately called his lawyer—anger flaring in his eyes. Cole's attorney, the formidable Ms. Valerie Chambers, immediately rose.

"Objection, Your Honor! This trial is about General Cole. Ms. McAllister and the others are not on trial here."

Judge Westwood looked thoughtful. "Ms. Chambers, I understand your concern. However, given the interconnected nature of the evidence, I will allow Mr. Rossi some latitude. Continue, Mr. Rossi, but stay on relevant ground."

Gio nodded, his eyes focused and intense. "Thank you, Your Honor. I intend to show the court that we cannot fully comprehend General Cole's role without exposing his connections with his co-conspirators."

The defense attorneys huddled together after being called in a hurry, visibly shaken, whispering urgently to each other.

Gio could see the ripple of anxiety passing through the group—Lansing (Agnes's attorney), Crane (Milton's attorney), Valerie (Cole's attorney), and Carlson (Vince's attorney)—all working for powerful clients who hadn't anticipated this escalation.

Smirking, knowing that the first blow definitely had an effect. To begin the dismantling of the cursed network, Gio displayed a scroll of paper, carefully unrolling it on the evidence stand for the jury to see, and he called Emily his first witness.

The scroll contained a detailed sketch Agnes had made, discovered in the hidden basement of the Old Mill on Wagner's tip. It depicted a figure resembling the murderer described by Agnes in Nicky's trial, and next to it was a notation of the plan they had concocted for his elimination.

"Miss Turner, tell us how you came across this sketch?" Gio asked.

"This," Emily said, pointing to the sketch, "was found in the basement of the Old Mill, a location tied to Mr. Vince and Mr. Milton. It's a representation of the murderer, a sketch from Agnes's own hand, visualizing their plan before it ever took place."

She pointed to Agnes, whose face betrayed a flicker of shock before she composed herself. The defense leaped into action.

Lansing, a seasoned attorney with a hawkish gaze, strode toward the witness stand where Emily was seated. His voice was laced with controlled contempt as he began his questioning.

"Ms. Turner," he began, his voice smooth but laced with skepticism, "you claim to have found this sketch in a hidden basement. Tell us, was this basement freely accessible?"

Emily remained calm. "No, it was hidden underneath a rusty old machine, and we gained access based on information from a reliable source."

Lansing chuckled, turning to the jury with raised eyebrows. "A hidden basement? Underneath an old machine? Are we in some kind of spy movie, Ms. Turner? Isn't it more likely that this 'evidence' was planted to frame Ms. McAllister?"

Emily didn't waver. "I, along with my team, conducted a thorough investigation, and everything checked out. The location and documents were consistent with records we gathered independently."

Lansing leaned in, his tone sharp. "And how convenient that this 'evidence' directly incriminates a prominent figure. You're a journalist, Ms. Turner. Isn't it your job to sensationalize stories for more readership?"

Gio rose swiftly. "Objection, Your Honor! The defense is attacking the witness's credibility without any basis."

Judge Westwood considered it, then nodded. "Sustained. Mr. Lansing, keep it relevant."

Lansing turned back to Emily, eyes narrowing. "Very

well. Tell us, Ms. Turner, why did you target Ms. McAllister? What proof do you have that she was behind any of this beyond your speculative sketch?"

Emily took a breath. "The sketch isn't speculative, Mr. Lansing. It's a blueprint of the murder, consistent with Ms. McAllister's role as described by other evidence."

Gio approached, calling up a transcript of Agnes's testimony from her first court appearance. "Ms. McAllister," Gio addressed Agnes directly, "you previously described a figure involved in Charles's murder—an 'intruder' with specific physical traits. Isn't it interesting," he said, holding up the sketch for the jury, "that the description you provided aligns perfectly with the sketch you drew yourself?"

Agnes's face tightened, but Lansing was quick on his feet. "Objection, Your Honor! This is purely circumstantial and doesn't prove Ms. McAllister's involvement."

Judge Westwood looked thoughtful. "Mr. Gio, you need more than just a sketch to establish Ms. McAllister's involvement beyond a reasonable doubt."

Gio nodded, prepared for this moment. "Understood, Your Honor. Let's proceed with more evidence."

As he continued presenting evidence, Crane, Milton's defense attorney, requested to cross-examine Gio himself. He approached Gio, his posture rigid, voice dripping with skepticism.

"Mr. Rossi," Crane began, "you seem quite invested in

tying Ms. McAllister, Mr. Vince, and Mr. Milton to this case. Isn't it possible that your focus on them is clouding your objectivity?"

Gio didn't miss a beat. "I'm focused on finding justice, Mr. Crane. The facts have led us here, and it's my duty to reveal those facts, even if they involve powerful people."

Crane smirked. "Interesting. And this *duty* of yours—does it include using speculative evidence to draw wild conclusions? Surely, you must understand the weight of what you're accusing Ms. McAllister and others of. This isn't just about General Cole anymore. You're making baseless accusations against respected individuals."

Gio felt the weight of the room's gaze. "I understand exactly what's at stake, Mr. Crane. And I wouldn't be standing here if I didn't have the evidence to back my claims."

"Then let's see it," Crane pressed, turning to the judge. "I request that the prosecution provide clear, indisputable proof of their intent."

Judge Westwood nodded, his eyes sharp as he looked at Gio. "Mr. Gio, the defense makes a fair point. You'll need solid evidence to continue implicating Ms. McAllister and others."

"Very well, Your Honor," he addressed the judge, "in light of the revelations we've just heard, and what we are about to reveal, I request that Agnes McAllister, Milton, and Vince be formally added as co-defendants."

The tension in the room ratcheted up upon seeing Gio's readiness. Finishing his statement, he called Wagner to the stand, whose stoic, lined face betrayed years of loyalty turned to regret. Wagner's mere stride sent chills down Agnes, Vince, and Milton's spines as they immediately jolted forward, murmuring something to their attorneys.

The courtroom erupted. The defense attorneys huddled quickly, whispering, their faces pale as they realized the full impact of Gio's request. They glanced at their clients, each of whom sat in stunned silence, faces tight with fear.

Lansing stood, his face red with anger. "Your Honor, this is unprecedented! We need time to prepare if this case is to be expanded in such a drastic manner. We weren't prepared for such witnesses."

Judge Westwood looked contemplative, and for a tense moment, the entire room held its breath. Finally, she nodded.

"Mr. Lansing is correct. The defense will be granted two days to prepare. I caution everyone," he said, turning to the gallery, "that this trial is of serious consequence and will proceed with full consideration of all implicated parties."

With the gavel's crack, she adjourned the court, giving the defense the time they needed. Gio and his team returned to their strategy, fine-tuning their approach for what would be the defining chapter of the trial.

Two days later, the courtroom was packed to capacity. Agnes, Milton, and Vince sat beside their attorneys, tension radiating from them. They were now active defendants, and

Gio could see the strain in their eyes as they prepared for battle. Judge Westwood settled in her seat and addressed the jury.

"Ladies and gentlemen, remember this: the defendants seated before you are innocent until proven guilty. Your role is to assess the facts presented—without prejudice, without speculation. Justice does not tolerate haste, nor does it excuse any rush to judgment. The verdict you deliver will shape lives—do not take this responsibility lightly."

And so, the court was in session, and Wagner's account provided a firsthand recounting of the meetings Agnes had led, detailing her directives and the lengths she went to in concealing her involvement in Charles's murder.

"Mr. Wagner," Gio began, "you were one of Charles's disciples, privy to his inner circle. Did Ms. McAllister explicitly discuss plans to harm Charles?"

Wagner nodded, his voice filled with remorse. "Yes, she did. She instructed us to make it look like an accident, and she recruited General Cole to execute the plan. As you can see on the scroll, the details of the murder were elaboratively recorded beforehand."

A murmur went through the courtroom as Lansing objected furiously, "This is unsubstantiated hearsay, Your Honor!"

Judge Westwood held up her hand as she skimmed through the documents Gio handed to the court—documents containing analysis of the professionals matching the writing on the scroll with Agnes, Milton, and Vince's writing, along with Wagner's proof of his involvement in the organization. "I'll allow it, given the defendant's documented presence at these meetings."

Lansing's composure slipped, and he fired back at Wagner. "And yet, Mr. Wagner, you conveniently turn against Ms. McAllister now? Aren't you simply covering for your own involvement?"

Wagner's voice was steady. "I take responsibility for my actions, but I won't let Miss Agnes walk free while others suffer for her decisions."

Valerie stood up, her voice rigid with years of experience as she cross-examined Wagner. "Mr. Wagner, I ask you— why now? Why come forward after all these years? Could it be that your conscience finally started to weigh on you? Or maybe you saw a way to secure yourself immunity? How convenient that you can't corroborate these meetings, these supposed 'plans!' Is this all just an attempt to save yourself?"

"Immunity or not, Ms. Chambers, what matters here is the evidence—the accounts that align perfectly with this so-called conspiracy. Your client is implicated by his own actions, not by the words of a single witness."

The defense team regrouped, visibly shaken. Crane, Milton's attorney, took a desperate turn, trying to paint Wagner's testimony as revenge, but Wagner's credibility held strong. Lansing attempted to discredit Gio's other evidence, but each one stood firm, reiterating their accounts with unshakable conviction. Each piece of evidence Gio and others had gathered up till now was presented with calculated precision that strengthened their case even more. With each blow, the faces of the defendants turned pale—as if their souls had been snatched from their bodies.

Cornered and fearful of the consequences of losing the case, Lansing changed his aim towards the jury—trying to intimidate and manipulate them, but Judge Westwood was quick to notice his dirty tactics. As Lansing took his seat, Judge Westwood addressed the jury.

"It is the solemn duty of this court to ensure that truth is not obscured by power or privilege. Today, let each voice be heard and let each piece of evidence bear the weight it deserves. We will proceed with deliberation, not intimidation."

A smile of victory curved upon each member of Gio's team, but Gio knew he had one last blow to deal—the closing statement. He stood before the jury, his presence commanding, his voice calm yet deeply resonant. The weight of the trial hunched over his shoulders, but Gio's gaze was unwavering as he looked each juror in the eye.

"Ladies and gentlemen of the jury," he began, his tone laced with sincerity, "we have seen the lengths to which these defendants went to manipulate, deceive, and destroy. We've laid bare the web of lies that has ensnared not just one life but many. In these past days, you've heard about the power wielded with ruthless intent, about how trust was twisted to serve ambition, and about a network of influence that, until now, thought itself untouchable."

He paused, letting his words sink in, drawing the room's attention into his focused stillness.

"The defendants in this case had wealth, status, and authority. They could have chosen to use those gifts to uplift and protect their communities, to better the lives of those around them. But instead, they chose a different path. They believed their position made them untouchable—that their power gave them the right to decide who deserved to live and who could be silenced. They believed the justice system would shield them because of their status, because of the privilege they've held for so long."

He turned to the jury, his voice carrying a mixture of gravity and hope. "But today, you have the power to prove them wrong. You have the power to show that justice does not bend to power or wealth. The defendants seated here didn't just commit crimes; they broke the trust of this community. They acted with a certainty that they would evade justice, believing their power could overshadow the law. But today, we are here to remind them—and the world—that justice is not blind to influence."

His eyes softened, a flicker of weariness visible. "In delivering your verdict, you're not just upholding justice for Charles Blackwood. You're making a stand—for integrity, for truth, and for every person who's had to live in the shadows of those who use power to oppress. I urge you, for the sake of every innocent life touched by these people, to find them guilty. Every piece of evidence, every witness's account, points us to the truth. Justice demands clarity, and today, it demands a reckoning. Let today be the day that the innocent find peace and the guilty finally pay the price."

The silence that followed was absolute. The jury seemed to hold their collective breath, the weight of his words heavy upon them.

Lansing stood from the defense table, ready to deliver her closing statement.

"Look around you. These are people who have given everything to their careers and to this community. And what do they get in return? Accusations, assumptions—all because someone chose to make them scapegoats in a crime they did not commit. My client's life is at stake here—her family, her legacy, her very dignity. Think carefully before you make an irreversible decision. Don't let a few coincidences blind you to a lifetime of integrity."

Finally, before letting the jury go, Judge Westwood's voice resounded one more time in the walls that upheld justice.

"Members of the jury, the weight of truth rests on your shoulders. The evidence has been presented, and both the prosecution and defense have made their case. But now, it is up to you to decide. Remember that each verdict, each answer, affects real lives. As you deliberate, let integrity guide your judgment, and let justice—true justice—be served."

After hours of deliberation, the jury returned, their expressions solemn but resolute. The judge called the court to order as the lead juror, a middle-aged woman with steady eyes, stood to deliver the verdict.

"For the charge of conspiracy to commit murder against Charles Blackwood," she said, "we find General Cole, Agnes McAllister, Mr. Milton, and Mr. Vince guilty."

A collective sigh swept through the room. Agnes clenched her fists, her face ashen with the realization that her power had finally crumbled. Milton sat stoically, his expression unreadable, while Vince's face twisted with barely concealed rage.

Judge Westwood nodded solemnly, her voice heavy as she declared, "The court finds the defendants guilty on all counts. Sentencing will follow shortly."

At that moment, Gio felt an immense sense of relief wash over him. He looked at Nicky, her eyes bright with unspent tears, the weight of months of accusation finally lifting from her shoulders. Agnes strolled by Gio, staring at him with a deathly glare in her eyes.

"Miss McAllister, you posed quite an intense question when everything began. About justice. And today, justice has been served, don't you think?" Gio sneered.

"You played well, Giuseppe Rossi. But don't think our ending would be defined by these walls. Every wall can be crumbled—even justice's," Agnes retorted.

"Life is all about choices, Miss McAllister. You had the strength to make the choices that led you here, but do you have the strength to live through the consequences of those choices?" Gio asked, meeting Agnes's gaze.

"We'll see," her voice faded as she walked away.

As the courtroom cleared, Gio found himself alone in the echoing silence, standing at the front of the empty benches, absorbing the events that had just unfolded. Outside the tall windows, the late afternoon sun cast long shadows across the room, illuminating the dust that floated softly through the air.

Nicky approached him, her steps light yet sure. "It's over," she said softly, her voice a mixture of relief and gratitude. "Thank you, Gio. For everything."

Gio nodded, a faint smile breaking through his exhaustion. "It was justice," he replied, his voice steady. "You deserve a chance to move forward—without these accusations looming over you."

They stood in silence for a moment, each lost in thought, the gravity of the trial still settling.

Finally, Nicky offered her hand, and Gio took it, feeling the warmth of her gratitude and hope in her grip. They turned to leave the empty courtroom, walking toward the doors as equals in both victory and struggle. Behind them, the dust continued to settle, caught in the golden light, as if even the room itself was at peace.

As they stepped out into the world beyond, Gio felt a rare sense of closure. The fight for justice had been grueling, but it was finally over. The truth had prevailed, and with it, a new chapter had begun—not only for him but for every life that had been tainted by deception.

Amidst the echo of their footsteps, Gio's mind drifted back to the time when Nicky was on trial—the beginning of everything, and today, the verdict she received *'Not guilty'* sounded just in his head.

www.ingramcontent.com/pod-product-compliance
Lightning Source LLC
La Vergne TN
LVHW021808060526
838201LV00058B/3291